PRAISE FOR
THE PAPER GARDEN

"Vance's stories, at their best, are immersive and gripping."
—*Publishers Weekly*

"Vance's stellar debut is a beautiful original offering. These stories find power in their strangeness, in their unwillingness to be easily reduced. There is blood and there is also tenderness and healing, this is a special work."
—**Nana Kwama Adjei-Brenyah, author of** *Friday Black*

"I loved Caitlin Vance's debut collection of stories and fractured fairy tales for its sensibility, which is simultaneously strange, angry, funny, tender, and wisely (and wryly) perceptive. Her characters (so often abandoned by parents or struggling with unreliable partners or the mentally ill) are compelling in their survival strategies. Without being Pollyanna—or slipping too wholly into the ever-present darkness of the world—they come out on top simply by making it to the end of their own remarkable stories."
—**Debra Spark, author of** *The Pretty Girl*

"These haunting and hilarious tales expose the fissures, absurdities, and inconsistencies in the stories we're told and the stories we tell ourselves. Whether the subject is an old parable, the haunted home of a troubled couple, the digressive answers penned into an intake form by a woman anxiously awaiting treatment, Vance's strange and often brutal worlds are signed with human, horror, and beauty."
—**Jessica Alexander, author of** *Dear Enemy*

I0587947

THE PAPER GARDEN

stories by

Caitlin Vance

7.13 Books
Brooklyn

Printed in the United States of America

First Edition
1 2 3 4 5 6 7 8 9

Cover art by Gigi Little
Edited by Hasanthika Sirisena

ISBN (paperback): 978-1-7361767-0-2
ISBN (eBook): 978-1-7361767-1-9
Library of Congress Control Number (LCCN): 2020953031

TULIPS

THE HOUSE ACROSS THE street was dark. It looked as if it had burned down and someone had re-built it using ash and tar and human bones. Small pieces of wood crumbled off it like Play-Doh, and windows were cracked. The grass was too tall, so that you had to look very closely to see the small garden of flowers bordering the house. I was six years old and I thought all the spiders in the world must hide there in winter. I thought there must be demons inside, plotting with maps and charts to trick people into coming in. For those first few days after my mother and I had moved in with my grandma in Coeur d'Alene, Idaho from across town, I watched the house, waiting to see a candle flicker or a hand drag across a window, but there was nothing.

On a summer evening not long after we moved to Grandma's, the sun hummed over the Earth's surface, so that there was a pressure, little hands pushing everything down, little bees filling space with white noise. The whole world felt tired and the sun scorched the ends of my hair, turning it to straw. I sat in the gravel of the front yard petting our cat, watching the house. A car pulled up after days of no sign of life; a man and a woman stepped out of it. The man went inside right away while the woman stayed, fiddling with things in the back seat. She was wearing a long dress like a river. Her hair was brown like mine, and braided, longer than any hair I'd ever seen. When she spotted me from across the street, she smiled the way I might smile if I'd finally made it to Disneyland. A cavity in my chest filled quickly with warm liquid. She picked up a paper grocery bag with something shiny sticking out of it, and came to me.

"Hello," she said, glowing.

I thought of a dream I'd had: I was in bed and couldn't speak or move. I stared up at the woman.

"What a pretty girl you are," she said, digging in her paper bag and pulling out the shiny thing, which was a necklace with a huge cross on the end. "I've just come from a church conference. The pastor gave everyone one of these to hang around their necks. It's nice to have God's love so close to your heart." She touched her own cross, which hung exactly at her heart and caught the sun, so that the orange of it stung right into my eyes. "I have one left over, but no daughter of my own to give it to. You look like you might like it." She hung the extra necklace over me. "My name's Scarlett and that man is my husband, Daniel." She pointed behind her at the house. "Do you have a name?"

I kept looking at her heart. The necklace was heavy, and I was small, and the cross hung closer to my belly button than my heart. "Saige," I said, so quietly she must have barely been able to hear me over the sound of a bouncing basketball up the street.

Scarlett went back to her house and I sat in the yard, thinking about this cross around my neck, about whether I should tear it off and bury it in the gravel, whether it was evil and Scarlett was evil and something in that house wanted me doomed. But I also thought maybe Scarlett had fallen into this house accidentally, that she didn't know it was evil, and that she was even sent here by God to save it. The way she spoke to me, her voice soft like petals, and the way she gave me this necklace, made me want to believe in her. The sun hung lower and I went inside.

I found my mother where I often found her that summer: in her rocking chair near the window, just looking out. She was wrapped in an afghan she had made back when she did things like that, back when she did anything at all. My mother was twenty-three. My best friend in first grade, Abigail, had a sister who was twenty-two. My mother was thin all over and had dusty hair she kept tied up with an old ribbon. She wore dresses in different shades of brown, like paper bags holding the sticks of her body together.

My father had left her a few months before I met Scarlett for the first time. He simply told my mother there was someone else and drove off. She hadn't told me yet, but kept saying he was away on business. My father was a trucker. I knew he wasn't coming back, because his trips never lasted as long as two months, and besides, I'd overheard my mother telling my grandma about it. Still, I imagined him driving along the coast, watching seagulls fly and waves crash out the window all the way to California. I'd never been to the ocean. I didn't know how to tell my mother I thought she was a liar.

Shortly after my father left, my grandmother showed up at our apartment with a U-Haul and a bundle of trash bags. She said it was time for an intervention, and when I asked what that meant, she said my mother just needed a little help right now, that's all. My mother sat in her rocking chair without a word while Grandma carefully inspected each item in the apartment, scrunched her nose, and scrubbed the item with a rag before cramming it into the truck.

When my parents were together, my father worked and my mother stayed at home taking care of me. A lot of mothers in Coeur d'Alene did this; childcare was too expensive to make having a job worth it. My mother dropped out of high school to give birth to me, the baby she'd conceived in the backseat of a blue Toyota with one brown door. When my father was actually away on business, things were different. My mother taught me to bake all kinds of cookies, draw bubble letters, and play "Happy Birthday" on the keyboard. She gave me a special Bible for kids and read to me while I sat on her lap, examining the patterns in her afghans and knitted scarves.

"Mom, I met a new lady," I said to my rocking mother. "She lives in the scary house. Is she bad? She gave me a necklace." I held it up for her to inspect. I knew she'd seen the whole thing out the window.

"How should I know?" she asked. She went to the kitchen and pulled a can of tomato soup out of the cupboard. "Saige," she said, "Come help me stir the soup for dinner."

Even though she didn't do much else that summer, my mother still tucked me into bed and sang to me each night. She had a beautiful singing voice, better than anyone's at church. More like an angel than a human. She'd been in her high school choir before she got me in her belly. Once I asked her why she didn't join the church choir, but she just said she didn't want to talk about it. After she finished her song to me each night, she'd remind me to say my prayers to Jesus and leave my door open a crack in case I needed her. Our cat perched on the window and looked out.

One night, after she left, I snuck out of Grandma's "office," where I slept, into the hallway. I spied on her through the crack she left in her bedroom door, careful not to make any noise because my grandma was across the hall in her own room, probably reading some book from the dollar bin.

My mother sat in bed, her eyes streaked with the Vaseline she used to take off her make-up. She was sifting through old photographs. I imagined what they might be: Dad hiking on the Olympic Peninsula, Dad drinking a beer outside a tent at Priest Lake, Dad holding me as a baby, so small my cross necklace would have reached the ground.

The next morning while my grandmother was out grocery shopping, the doorbell rang. My mother was in the habit of not answering the door, letting the sound of the bell pass over her body like the gong in meditation. It would end, and whoever it was would leave her with me and the cat and the blank space that used to hold my father. But this time the person at the door did not leave; they kept ringing the bell. Finally, my mother moved to the door. I crept up on the first stair, so the wall would hide me from whoever it was. I peeked out slightly.

"Hello," said Scarlett, smiling.

There she was on the porch. She stood very straight and tall, as if little strings from the sky were tugging her up. The cross hung from her neck, and she held a plate of green Jell-O with pears. "My name is Scarlett. I live across the street with my husband, Daniel. Your mother told me you were coming to stay here, and I wanted to personally welcome you to the neighborhood. I made you some Jell-O; I hope you like it." She handed the plate to my mother.

"Thank you," said my mother, taking the plate much too slowly, her body forming a wall between Scarlett and the inside of the house. I wondered why she couldn't be more polite and invite her in for cookies. Was it because she was jealous Scarlett still had a husband?

"It's a pleasure to meet you. I already met your daughter, Saige. I gave her a necklace like mine; I hope you don't mind. She's such a sweet girl. Doesn't talk much, though. Is she very shy?"

Adults always called me shy.

"She's always been quiet," said my mother. I thought my mother had always been quiet, too.

"By the way," Scarlett said, her voice getting faster, "I hope this isn't too personal of a question, but are you a Christian?"

My mother took me to Holy Spirit Baptist Church every Sunday. My grandma said she had only started going to church when she got pregnant with me, and she made my father go with her, even though he never prayed a day in his life and didn't even accept Jesus Christ as his Lord and Savior.

A leaf drifted down from the sky and landed on Scarlett's shoulder. She brushed it off, twitching her nose a bit.

"Yes, I'm a Christian," said my mother.

"Oh, good. I am so happy for you." Scarlett's face filled with a bit more color. "You see, I run a Bible study for the children in the neighborhood. I've been doing it since Daniel and I got married and moved here three years ago. The children come over once a week, and we sing songs and recite verses, and I teach Bible stories. It's so good for the children to get to know each other and to share God's love. I would be thrilled to invite Saige to join, if it's okay with you."

I clenched my teeth.

My mother crossed her arms, gripping her sweater closer around her. "That's very kind of you, but I don't know...we go to a Baptist church, and I like that, but there are so many different denominations. I'm not sure if I want her learning about God when I can't see what she's learning."

Scarlett didn't respond right away.

My mother said, "Just, you know, I don't want to confuse her. Things are so complicated as is."

The color in Scarlett's face faded slightly. "Oh, okay...Of course, I understand," she said. "Things are very complicated. Well, if you change your mind, you know where to find me. The invitation is always there. Your mom told me about your situation, you know. I'm sure it's all very hard on Saige. It might help her to have some activities." Her eyes moved in my direction. I pulled my face back right away, hiding it completely behind the wall. She knew I was here. I wondered if it was because she snuck around too, spying on people and hiding in corners.

"Nice to have met you," my mother managed to say. Scarlett, I'm sure, smiled before turning away down the steps. The door shut, and I scurried up the stairs and into Grandma's office/my room.

I thought all day about the Bible study. I set up the stuffed animals Grandma gave me on the futon, draping the cross necklace around my biggest bear, and taught them about God. I tried to explain everything.

"A long time ago," I said, "God made everything, bears and

people and flowers, and it was all beautiful. He lives in Heaven in the sky, I think floating around on clouds all the time. He made Heaven too. Everything was perfect, but there was an angel Lucifer who wanted to be bad, so he left Heaven and created Hell. Even though Lucifer lives in Hell, which is underground, he is always coming to Earth and filling it up with evil and temptation."

The animals looked worried.

"But don't worry!" I said. "You can escape Lucifer and his evil friends. The only way is to trust Jesus Christ, that's God's son, as your savior, because He is full of love and wants the best for us."

One of the bears asked why we should trust Jesus, not God, when God is the one who made everything in the first place.

"They're the same person," I said, "and there is also the Holy Ghost. He's part of it too."

The bear wanted to know how three things could be one thing. The rabbit wanted to know if you dug a deep enough hole, would you get to Hell. I decided there was much more work for me to do before I could go on teaching. My mom never wanted to answer my questions, but I was sure Scarlett would.

Scarlett spoke a sweet way to my mother. She loved us both, I was almost sure of it. Why had my mother said no to her? Was it because she figured anyone who lived in that house must be evil?

The next morning, Oscar was staring out my window at something. He always discovered the most interesting things. I looked out with a pair of binoculars my father had left behind. I adopted them as my favorite toy; with them I saw far away from the place I lived. On the sidewalk outside Scarlett's house, there was a white bucket with flowers sticking out of it. I ran down the stairs right away and, still in my pajamas, out the door and across the street. There were twelve flowers sticking out of the bucket, all different kinds: a tulip, a daffodil, a rose. There was a sign on the bucket that said "Flowers: 25 cents. Please be honest. God is watching." I looked around. No sign of anyone who could have put it here. I was touching the petals of the red tulip when I heard Scarlett.

"Good morning, Saige," she said. She startled me. Where did she come from? "What a pretty nightgown. What have you found there?"

I quickly took my hand off the tulip. She had on a sunhat over her braid today, with the widest brim and the longest ribbon I'd ever seen, like two halos.

"Beautiful flowers for beautiful girls," she said. "Which is your favorite? I bet it's that tulip."

I nodded, not making eye contact.

"I see they cost a quarter. Let me buy it for you," she said. Scarlett dropped the light silver coin into the bucket. It rattled in the bottom for a moment, and she handed me the tulip.

"Thank you," I managed to say.

"You're very welcome," she said, and patted me on the head. I felt the residue of her fingers there, like a hat of paper, for the rest of the day.

In the living room I stacked up colored blocks, building the tallest tower I could, trying to make it bigger than the piano my grandma bought at a garage sale when my mother was in high school. I hadn't heard her play since my father left. Like everything that was my mother's, it sat there, collecting dust.

"Mom, why can't I go to the Bible study?" I asked.

My mother sighed. "Because, Saige, we go to a Baptist church. I don't know that lady. I don't know what kind of church she goes to or what she believes. There are lots of churches: Mormon, Jehovah's Witness, Liberal Christian. She could believe anything: that we shouldn't celebrate Christmas, that Jesus was married, that Hell isn't real, that Noah's Ark never actually happened. You can't go; I'm sorry. But you can keep going to Sunday school with me."

"What's so good about Noah's Ark being true?" I asked. "Why did God want to flood the Earth, anyway? All those people died. And the cats, too."

"I can't answer that, honey," she said.

"Was it because people were bad?"

"Yes, because people are bad."

"I thought God was nice and the devil was mean."

"God is nice not to flood the Earth now," she said. Then she went away to feed Oscar.

Sometimes I wished God *would* flood the Earth. I wanted rain, so much that I'd float on top of it, a lake covering the whole Earth. I would have a raft, and I'd take all my best things on it with me: my cat, my binoculars, my tulip and my necklace. I'd splash myself to quiet the sun's loud rays.

That summer, my grandma had a lot of private conversations with my mother, which I often listened to even though I wasn't supposed to. This time, they were in my mother's room, and I crouched outside, my ear pressed against the closed door.

"You have to stop moping around," said my grandmother. "You have to do something. If not for yourself, then at least for Saige. She needs you."

"It's not like I'm doing this to hurt Saige," said my mother. "I'm not the one who left; he is. This isn't my fault."

"I know you're upset, but you need to push past that. Think of Saige. She'll—"

"She'll turn out like me?" Her voice was raised. "She'll drop out of school and get pregnant? That's what she'll do if I don't get out of my chair?"

"Oh, that's not what I meant," she said. "But I think it's time for you to get a job. What would you like to do? You used to love music—"

"Why did you tell that woman across the street all about my life?"

"Oh, stop it. She seems like a good person. She has a Bible study, you know, for children, and Saige—"

"Saige is not going to her Bible study."

There was a silence. "I think I need a glass of water," my grandmother said.

The floorboard creaked; my grandma was moving towards the door. I quietly scampered down the stairs and into the kitchen. I heard my grandma coming close behind me.

"Saige, were you listening?" she asked. She looked angry, but behind her anger I saw comfort in being able to take it out on me, a small child misbehaving, rather than on my mother.

"No," I said.

"Eavesdropping is wrong and lying is wrong. You should know that. Your mother wants—"

"My mom doesn't want to help me," I said.

"Saige!" she said, gasping. "Don't say those kinds of things about your mother."

"But it's true," I said, "and you just said lying is wrong. She doesn't want to get a job to buy food for me. I need to eat or I'll die! She is just like a demon wanting to kill all the people."

"Saige!" she said again. "That is extremely rude and is not true. Your mother is doing her best. I don't want to hear you say anything like that again. Children obey and respect their parents and you will do the same."

She washed my mouth out with soap and said no Jell-O for me. She went back upstairs to my mother, closing the bedroom door behind her.

I got the Jell-O out of the fridge and stuck all my fingers into it at once. I didn't even want to eat it; I didn't even like Jell-O. My mom said it was made out of cow's feet. I scooped up pieces of it and shoved them in my mouth. It was slippery, like little fishes about to die, not sure if they should swim down my throat or out my lips. I wondered if they took fish on Noah's Ark even though they could live underwater. I left the plate on the counter, most of the Jell-O still on it.

I went outside to my gravel, careful to close the door quietly behind me. My mother was not like she used to be. She had opened up the top of her head, and allowed the cloud that held her soul to float out. She was like the watercolor I painted and left out too long in the sun: she had dried up and faded out.

I noticed a sign on Scarlett's house that said, "Bible Study Tonight, 7 pm." That meant it was happening now, and that meant I was going, because even if my mother didn't want to help me, God would want to help me, and Scarlett would, too.

I made my way into Scarlett's overgrown yard and to her window. Peering in, I saw Scarlett standing beside an easel, attaching several felt shapes to it: a camel, a person, a boat. Four children I'd seen around the neighborhood sat in front of her, singing. A man came out of the kitchen, holding a tray of cookies. He looked right at me, and I ducked.

I was kneeling in their flower bed under the window; they would be so mad I was trampling their flowers. I noticed a tulip plant, and thought of the tulip Scarlett had bought me from the bucket.

"Hey there!" said the man, stepping out the door. "You must be Saige. Scarlett's told me all about you. I'm her husband, Daniel."

How did he know I was Saige? He looked like he was waiting for something, so I nodded.

"Nice to meet you, Saige. Would you like to come inside? We're having Bible study."

The hum of the setting sun got louder and higher-pitched, as if God had instructed an orchestra to begin the crescendo.

"Oh, that's right, your mother doesn't want you to come," he said. "Okay, I understand. Well, have a nice evening!" Daniel turned to leave, but Scarlett appeared in the doorway at just the right moment.

"Saige!" she said. "What are you doing out here alone? Where's your mother?"

"She's in the house with my grandma," I said.

"Oh, well, why don't you come inside? The two of them might like some time alone. Daniel made cookies!"

I realized I was actually going to go inside the house across the street, and my heart and stomach did a few somersaults around each other.

"I'll explain it to your mother later. It will be fine," she said.

Her eyes looked right into mine, like they were not just her eyes but mine as well, and everyone's. I felt like liquid as I stood up, dusted off my shorts, and followed Scarlett into the house.

"Scarlett," I said, "did you put those flowers in the bucket?"

"Of course not!" she said. "Don't be silly. I was just as surprised to see them there as you were. But they sure were beautiful."

She led me into the living room, where I sat by the other children.

The house looked normal, which seemed strange. There were couches, some photographs of Scarlett and Daniel's wedding, a few plants. A painting of a flower. A painting of a boat.

"Now, Saige, we were just discussing Noah's Ark," said Scarlett. "Do you know that story?"

I had heard the story, but I wasn't sure if that meant I knew it, the way you could know your address, or the color of your hair, or the name of your neighbor.

"Yes," I said.

"Do you like it?"

"Well," I said, scrunching my forehead, "I'm not sure. I don't know why God would want to kill all the people. I thought God was perfect and never sinned, and that's why we have to trust Him. My mom says he flooded the Earth because people are bad."

"Saige!" she said, shaking her head. She was looking directly and only at me, as if the other children had vanished. "People aren't bad. They sin, but that's just because they're imperfect. They're human. But they don't deserve to die." On the wall, I noticed a cross-stitched picture of Jesus hanging on the cross, and I liked how small and perfect the stitches were. "Some people believe stories like Noah's Ark are parables—they aren't true facts, but made-up stories intended to teach us lessons. Noah's Ark teaches us that we should obey God, or there will be consequences. But God doesn't want to kill everyone."

Daniel passed around the cookies. Everyone was eating; it seemed the lesson was over.

"I'm so glad you could make it to Bible study, Saige," Scarlett said. "Ever since I met you, I knew you were special. I knew you were one of God's favorite children."

"My pastor says God loves everyone," I said. The other kids smiled and nodded.

"Oh, He does!" she said. "The point is, Saige, we're so glad you could be here."

Daniel came over with his plate of cookies. "Scarlett made a special cookie just for you, Saige!" he said. He handed me a cookie shaped like a tulip.

I asked to use the bathroom.

"Yes, of course," Scarlett said. "There's one on this floor—just there to the left. You don't need to go upstairs. It's an awful mess!"

I nodded.

I crept around the whole floor, but could not find a bathroom. I knew Scarlett said not to go upstairs, but I couldn't help it. I tiptoed up and moved to the right.

Soft, violet light shone out of one door. I pushed it open and snuck inside.

This was not a bathroom at all, but some kind of room I had never seen before. Someone had stuck thousands of silver push pins into the walls. It seemed the person had been very careful about how they stuck each one in, as if the wall had skin and could feel pain. The pins made a picture of a tulip and a little girl's face. There was nothing else in the room, except for a tin box of pins in the middle of the floor.

I plucked a single pin out of the wall, a piece of the girl's mouth, and dragged it lightly over my hand.

I thought of the tulip Scarlett bought for me after planting the bucket there and waiting for me to come find it. I noticed the girl on the wall had big eyes, but that she looked only at the tulip, as if hiding from anyone who might see the picture. She was scared. Again, a cavity in my chest filled with hot liquid. This was my face, and Scarlett had stuck all these pins in the wall. It must have taken hours and hours, and she barely even knew me, and my mother would never do something like this. Why would Scarlett make this? Was Noah's Ark a real story or a fake story? Why didn't my mom want to get a job so she could buy more cans of soup for us? Where did my dad go, and why didn't he want to buy me soup? And if God was so nice, why would He let any of this happen? I was too tired to stand. I sat on the floor.

I heard the door creak open and quickly stuffed the pin into my pocket. Scarlett was standing there, hands on her hips. "Saige," she said, her voice a little less sweet than usual, "I told you not to come upstairs."

I opened my mouth to speak, but my voice got caught in my fear. I had to try a few times to get the sound to come out. "I'm sorry," I said, quietly. "I couldn't find the bathroom downstairs. I really couldn't find it." I was about to ask if I could ask a question, but was interrupted by a heavy sigh puffing out of Scarlett's mouth.

"You want to know why all these pins are in the wall," she said.

"Yes," I said. Scarlett had a way of knowing what I was thinking.

"I stuck them in," she said. "I've been working on it for the past few days. I bought thousands and thousands of pins. I studied a single tulip and a photograph I took of a little girl. I stuck the pins in one by one, slowly and deeply, thinking all the time about the girl and how happy she'd be when she saw it. I think I did a pretty good job, don't you?"

As she looked at me for approval, I noticed how long her eyelashes were, like legs of a wolf spider.

"You did a good job," I said. I didn't want to upset her, to find out what she turned into when provoked.

"And do you know whose face this is?" she asked, coming closer to me.

Yes, I knew whose face it was. I knew whose picture she had studied. I knew because I was always sneaking around, hiding behind doors and listening to conversations, spying. Scarlett was just like me, only she was older, so she had thicker curtains and sneakier tricks. She'd been watching all along.

"No," I said.

"Saige, it's your face," she said. "Don't you love it? I made it for you. It was supposed to be a surprise, for later, but you found it on your own. I guess God wanted you to see it tonight."

"When did you take the picture?" I asked.

"Never mind that," she said. "Saige, you're very special to me."

I wasn't sure what to say. "Thank you," I said.

"Saige," she said, moving still closer, "I see that you're unhappy. And I want to make you happy. Your grandmother told me about the trouble your mother is going through, and how she won't give you what you need."

She looked at me, as if waiting for me to tell her she was right. "My mom doesn't want to get a job," I said, "but my grandma says she's trying her best."

She shook her head like a disappointed teacher. "Saige, you deserve to have someone who loves you." Did she mean my mother didn't love me? My mother was sad, but she still kissed my forehead every night, and she still prayed for me, and she let my grandma scoop us up in the U-Haul, maybe because she thought it would be better for me. Scarlett sat down next to me and took my hand. "You see, I can't have children of my own. I have a condition. But if I could, I would love them so much I'd make them a new push-pin picture every day."

I was sorry she couldn't have children, and I wondered what kind of condition this was. I imagined a little demon in her belly, keeping all the babies away. "Scarlett," I asked, "why does God let bad things happen?"

Her face was closer to mine than it had ever been and I saw she had wrinkles. She was much older than my mother.

"You know, Saige," Scarlett said, slowly, and already I knew she wouldn't answer my question, "I think God brought us together for a reason. Sometimes children are born into bad homes, but it's not their fault. There are others out there who can help, who can take them away from those bad homes and care for them. And Saige, I want to help you."

She stroked my cheek with the backs of her fingers, rocking slowly back and forth, her eyes not really focused on anything. Then she stroked my hair, then my legs, then my stomach, beginning to hum.

I stood up. "I have to go now," I said. I moved towards the door as quickly as possible, not looking back at her.

I heard her say, in a voice like barnacles, "Saige, be careful of the choices you make. God will make you sorry."

As I hurried down the stairs, the sound of her voice grew legs and chased me, banging against the walls and floor like a stream of tumbling boxes. It was trying to pull me backwards to her, saying over and over "God will make you sorry, God will make you sorry." As I ran away, I planned what I would do.

I'd go home and help my grandmother wash the carrots and the bed sheets. I'd wash my nightgown I'd worn outside, my hair and my feet. I'd wash my mother's hair; I'd scrub and scrub until she begged me to stop because I was hurting her scalp. I'd wash my nightstand, which was dirty from the tulip I'd laid there days before. I'd wash my insides with gallons and gallons of water.

Then I'd leave. I'd scoop up everything I needed in a pillowcase: my cat, my binoculars, a few loaves of bread, the necklace, the pin, some of my mother's photos. I'd go towards the ocean, away from the screech of the sun, which, as it now dipped almost completely out of the sky, made the sound of a banshee's scream, muffled by the pillow God pressed over her mouth. I'd float into the ocean with the things in my pillowcase, holding the pin between two fingers, not wanting to keep it, but not wanting to toss it away because of what it might do to a fish.

Instead, I told my mom what happened. She stroked my hair, said everything would be okay, and sang me to sleep. She and I stayed at my grandma's a few more weeks, until she finally got that job at the music store. Then my grandma said we could move back home, and grandma would come over and babysit me for free when Mom needed it. During those last few weeks at my grandma's I mostly stayed inside coloring—not drawing, but coloring, so all I had to do was choose a crayon and fill in the shape, already there in such clear black lines. Oscar stayed close to me.

I peered out my window at Scarlett's house. One morning, I saw her place a white bucket filled with flowers on the sidewalk. She took the bucket away that evening, but it didn't look like any of the flowers were gone. A few times, I saw her walk out her door and take a few steps toward the street, only to stop dead for minutes in the middle of her lawn, as if thinking about something very confusing, before turning around and going back inside. I wondered what things she saw me do out her window.

The Bible study sign appeared the few more Tuesdays we were there. Whenever we went back to my grandma's house after that, I pulled my hood over my face for the walk from the car to the door. I didn't let myself look in that direction. Still, I felt Scarlett's eyes on me.

I finally made it to the ocean. My grandma took us on a camping trip there a few months later. Standing on the shore, my mind drifted back to Scarlett. Water had a way of pushing my thoughts along like clouds in quiet wind. I stuck my hand in my pocket and found Scarlett's pin in there, like a little demon scale or an angel's earring, depending on how you looked at it. I couldn't help but wonder what my life would have been like if I lived by the ocean instead of in the desert, if my cat had been a dog instead of a cat, if my mom had left instead of my dad. I told my mom some of these things but I'd never tell her that, although Scarlett was strange and scary, I had to wonder what my life would have been like if

I'd been Scarlett's daughter instead of my mother's. Probably it would have been part good and part bad, just like people were part good and part bad, and so was everything. I wondered if this included God. I looked out and saw where the water met the sky, like a blue sheet of paper folded and propped up against something else. I thought of Hell underground and Heaven in the sky, and I wondered if I floated out far enough, I could reach that sky and touch it, and touch the cloud God floated on, and say Hello.

A RED WINTER SHADOW

ON THE COLDEST MORNING of the year, when the breath escaped Margaret's mouth like a ghost, Margaret and James forgot to leave the water running. Their pipes froze, and no water at all came out when they turned on the faucets. It was a Friday in January, only a few days after New Year's, and people still carried around lofty ideas about hope and change, Margaret and James included. Margaret had quit smoking and James had quit eating so much candy. James had also told Margaret he wanted to give her an engagement ring, but that he wanted her to choose it herself at the store this weekend. He didn't know what kind of ring she would like, and did not want to impose his own aesthetic on her. Margaret appreciated this choice James was giving her, because she felt it was a small feminist gesture, but she also dreaded having to make a decision. The frozen water pipes did not fit with Margaret's expectations for the upcoming year or the beginning of her engagement. Nothing should be broken at a time like this.

Margaret and James lived on the second floor of a large, old house that had been divided into four apartments like chambers of the heart. The other three apartments had been empty the entire time they had lived in the building, because they were in need of renovation and deep cleaning. The landlord was drunk all the time and did not seem in a hurry to do this. Margaret and James had never been in any of the other apartments, which felt strange to Margaret, since they shared walls. Margaret and James were sealed off in their own little section of the big house. Their section was mostly updated, although it still had a broken oven, no heater, and several holes in the walls for insects to crawl through.

They called the plumber, but he would unfortunately be unable to come until Monday. "Sorry," the landlord texted. He also said the couple was welcome to use the bathroom in Apt. 1 downstairs.

"Dick," James said. James always dealt with the landlord, whose weird gaze and jokes about sex bothered Margaret. James went to get the keys. James and Margaret took care of each other. They were a team.

James went to work without taking a shower, which surely bothered him a little, because he generally took good care of his hygiene (unlike Andrew, the insane veteran who was Margaret's ex-fiancé). But James was a preschool teacher, and he said the children would not mind terribly or even notice if he skipped one shower. Margaret was in her first year as an assistant professor of Gender Studies, an accomplishment for someone in her mid-thirties. Margaret's father had always said she'd accomplish great things in her career, regardless of her gender. She was currently still on winter break. She planned to spend the day at home revising an article about feminism that she hoped to publish in an academic journal. She needed to publish more articles to get tenure. She needed to publish more articles to remain accomplished. Although she did not plan to leave the house all day, she still insisted on showering downstairs, as she was a woman who measured her self-worth based not only on her professional achievements, but also on how she looked, even on days when she saw no one. It bothered Margaret that her personal feelings did not always line up with her intellectual beliefs. But she couldn't help it.

After James left, Margaret put her towel and her bottles of soap and shampoo in a plastic bag. The keyring for Apartment 1 had about a dozen keys. Margaret could not imagine the reason for this.

She had to go outside and down a staircase to access the down-stairs apartment. She tried the main door first. None of the keys on the keyring opened the main door, or at least, they didn't work when she tried. Perhaps she was not inserting the keys correctly. In general, she worried she did not do enough things correctly. She was in a sour mood due to the water being broken, and became more and more annoyed with each failure to open the door. She went to the side door. During the summer, wasps had built a nest above the door, but all the wasps were now dead in the cold. She had success with this door.

The apartment felt much larger than it looked from the outside and it was very open, with a huge kitchen and two living rooms. The landlord or previous tenants had left some items there: two large mirrors, a nude painting of a woman, and a large sculpture of a man's head on the mantle. Margaret turned on the main light, which was attached to a ceiling fan that began to rotate. Its blades sliced the cold air and stirred up something that had been lying in the apartment, very still as if sleeping, for a long time. The blades clicked as they cut the air, like a record player still on after the album's end, rhythmically skipping over the silence, waiting for someone to come change it.

The ceiling fan made Margaret uncomfortable, so she walked away from it, into the bathroom. She lifted the toilet seat and saw that it was covered with a thick layer of dirt. Margaret did not like dirt, and furthermore, she liked everything to be in perfect order all the time. She had rituals that made her wonder if she were insane. Margaret wiped the dirt off with a wad of damp toilet paper, then washed her hands. The toilet seat now looked clean, but was obviously not clean, as there were no cleaning products there for her to use. She hovered above the seat, and winced as she urinated.

When she looked down, she noticed that she was once again bleeding, though she could not possibly be menstruating again already. She never had irregular bleeding like this until she started dating James. Other people had irregular bleeding for lots of different reasons, but she knew hers was related to the harmful strain of HPV that James had given her.

James's ex-girlfriend had cervical cancer, something James had neglected to tell Margaret until they'd been together for several months. He waited until she was in love with him, when she would not be able to reject him because of this. *Everyone has HPV*, Margaret had thought at first, and this was basically true, but not everyone had this kind. James tried to convince Margaret that he did not understand the severity of cervical cancer or its link to HPV. He also tried to employ a bizarre line of reasoning in which Margaret was a magical, beautiful creature who was immune to the same infections that harmed other women.

Margaret had gone to the doctor a year ago when James told her about the cervical cancer. She had an abnormal pap smear, but no cancer, at least not yet. The doctor told her to keep an eye on the bleeding, and to come back frequently for check-ups. But Margaret had not gone back since, and didn't plan to anytime soon. She did not like doctors. They could tell if you were dying, and they would let you know.

Margaret washed her hands again and let the thoughts of bleeding seep out of her mind. She did not think of the bleeding except when she saw it. She mostly thought of how nice James was to her now, unlike the other men she had dated. His bad behavior from the past did not fit with Margaret's current idea of James. She looked into the bathtub. It was dirty, and filled with several insects. They were mostly dead, but one was apparently still alive. It lay on its back with its legs kicking and struggling in the air, gasping. Margaret shuddered. She did not like insects any more than she liked dirt. She turned the water on and washed them down the drain. She heard a faint screaming from the old pipes, as if the dead insects were in pain. She heard a deep breathing from the other room, or at least, her mind told her she heard it. She had had hallucinations her whole teenage and adult life, mostly auditory hallucinations of creatures breathing or growling under her bed while she tried to sleep. It used to disturb her, but she was used to it now.

Margaret's father had insisted that she did not have hallucinations, but just saw and heard things other people couldn't. "You were born with the umbilical cord wrapped around your neck," he had said, "so I knew you'd be special." After Margaret's mother died when she was four, her father raised her to believe in ghosts, but to not be unnecessarily afraid. Some ghosts were good and some were bad, he explained to her, just like people. Margaret's father taught her that the way to get rid of ghosts she didn't want was to burn sage next to her bed at night. She found this never worked for her. She learned to ignore or at least tolerate the ghosts or hallucinations, whatever they were.

Margaret did not go out of her way to notice ghosts now, but she did sometimes feel them. She kept this secret from most people, for fear of ridicule, even though she did not personally believe the idea of ghosts was any stranger than, for example, God.

Margaret tried the hot water and it did not work, so she stuck with the cold, which barely dripped down in a tiny stream. *Pain is beauty,* she thought to herself, and considered whether or not she believed this. She removed her clothing and hung it over the open bathroom door rather than putting it on the dirty floor or counter. She got into the shower despite the dirt, which she could feel contaminating the soles of her feet. She thought about the strangeness of contaminating oneself in the shower, where the objective was to become clean.

The bathroom was set up so that she could see her whole body in the mirror as she showered. Her own apartment had just one small mirror, in which she could see herself only from the waist up. She was now faced with her entire naked body, which looked thinner than it had a year ago, but still not how she wanted it to look. When she was a child, her father had noticed her looking in mirrors too often and for too long. He gave her a warning. "Some women go crazy that way," he had said. "I don't want you to be crazy." Margaret's solution to this was to avoid full-length mirrors.

She never developed an eating disorder. But she spent just as much time looking in small mirrors, at her face, applying the same makeup over and over every time she used the restroom, for fear that it may have faded and her imperfections would show through.

Margaret watched her body shiver and hunch over in the mirror as she showered. She shaved her legs every day, and so she shaved now, although her legs were covered in goosebumps and it stung when she moved the razor blade across them. She was careful, but still made a tiny cut on her ankle. The blood flowed down the drain with the insects.

As she leaned her head back to rinse the conditioner out of her hair, trying not to let it drip onto her back for fear of developing acne there, she was forced to move her gaze from the mirror to the open bathroom door. Through the door, the ceiling fan still rotated. Some little dangling strings with beads on the ends clicked against each other. The fan reminded Margaret of time, how she'd always thought of weeks and months and years as circles, not lines. The fan rotated again and again, oblivious, as if the miracle of this order meant nothing to it. The strings disrupted this order. Margaret wanted them to just hang there, straight and still like icicles, but they insisted on being affected by the fan's rotation, and spun about like the stupid swing ride at the fair, clicking. The sun shone bright through the bathroom window like a voyeuristic intruder. The water burned in its coldness, a knife-like icicle being thrust into her. She shut the water off. She shuddered again.

The towel on her cold skin felt like another razor blade. She tried to dry off quickly, and forgot about the cut on her ankle. "Fuck," she said when she noticed the red stain on the towel. She blinked her eyes in rapid succession, a nervous habit she'd developed in childhood. Each time she blinked, it was like a blank slate: she was looking at the world with new eyes. She would do this when she stared at her father's framed picture of her dead mother, a woman she could imagine to be perfect because she did not really remember her. Margaret wanted desperately to be like this perfect woman.

As she put her clothes back on, she thought about how different it was the last time she got engaged, without rings (for ideological reasons), to Andrew, who ended up throwing himself off his rich mother's third-story balcony in a psychotic episode on Christmas. He didn't die, but broke many bones in his back and neck, which necessitated a dangerous surgery and several months with a back brace. That Christmas, Margaret had gone to another state to visit her father for what she knew would be the last time, because of how bad his lung cancer had gotten. When Margaret heard what Andrew had done, she got in the car to drive back, saying goodbye to her father. When Margaret walked into the hospital room and saw Andrew lying there in a crumpled heap, slurring meaningless words through a mouth of broken teeth, she knew the relationship was over. If Andrew wanted to die, he clearly didn't want to be with Margaret. But it didn't end right away, because Margaret held a great sense of guilt inside her and also drew satisfaction from the fantasy that she could save someone. Andrew was now living alone in a weird house he built deep in the woods, not working, shooting deer and squirrels for food, and playing guitar.

Andrew would accidentally refer to the period after his suicide attempt as "After I died" rather than "After I tried to die," which had worried Margaret. She would lie awake while Andrew slept, trying to pinpoint what exactly it was that had changed in him. It was true, some part of him had died, and something worse had taken its place. Andrew would jolt straight up in his sleep and scream. Margaret stopped having sex with him.

Since that time, Margaret had developed a new compulsion of repeating the phrase "I'm going to kill myself" approximately every sixty seconds in her mind. This was automatic: she did not do it on purpose, and she could not stop. She also developed involuntary, violent daydreams in which, instead of slitting her wrists, she cut her left arm off with an axe, then cut her right arm off as well, although her left arm was already detached and could not possibly hold an axe. It bothered her that this daydream did not make sense.

At times when she felt particularly anxious, such as now, shivering in this cold and obviously-haunted apartment, these thoughts and daydreams increased in frequency until Margaret developed a piercing headache.

Margaret hurried out of the apartment, turning the ceiling fan off before she left.

James came home from work while Margaret sat on the edge of the bed, her arms outstretched in front of the space heater, the electric blanket he'd bought her to help with menstrual cramps on her lap. She was not menstruating, but was bleeding, she suddenly remembered, and she also felt very cold. "I've been sitting here for hours," she said, sharpness in her voice. "I can't get warm." He sat next to her and kissed her cheek. "I accomplished nothing on my article today. It's too cold," she said. Margaret knew James thought she was too hard on herself. He probably thought now, since she was on a break, that she should take it easy, but she did not see it this way.

"It's okay," he said, stroking her hair. "How was the shower downstairs?"

"Bad. The hot water doesn't work, only the cold. And everything's dirty." She did not tell him about the ceiling fan or the breathing. She couldn't find the words to describe these things. She blinked in rapid succession. James always noticed when she did this. None of her other boyfriends had ever noticed. It was important to her that James noticed.

"Are you okay?" he asked her. He held her hand.

"Yes, I'm sorry. It was just really cold. I'm still cold." James rubbed her arm. She thought of a story her father had told her the last time she saw him: that shortly after her mother died, when his anger problems were at their worst, he had gotten upset with Margaret for being too needy, grabbed her, and dislocated her arm. He took her to the hospital and they fixed her. *I've never been so sorry for anything*, he had said. *It was the last bad thing I did.* Margaret could think of a lot of bad things her father did, but she did not remember this story actually happening.

"Well, in that case," said James, "I think I'll wait until tomorrow. I need to look good for the jewelry store." He smiled at her, then got another blanket from the closet and wrapped it around her shoulders. He kissed her. She felt lucky, and wondered if she should be less mean to him.

The next morning was even colder than the last, and Margaret and James took several minutes to get out of bed. It was painful to remove the blankets and walk away from the space heater into the kitchen to make coffee.

James was afraid of dark and unknown spaces, so Margaret entered the abandoned apartment first. James switched on the main light, so that the ceiling fan began once more to rotate. Margaret felt like a sharp, metal instrument inside her was beginning to turn, catching her organs on its edges and pulling them in the wrong directions. James put his hands over his ears as if he heard a loud screaming. "I do *not* like it in here," he said.

"Exactly," said Margaret.

James got in the shower, turned on the cold water, and screamed. "I don't think I can do this," he said. "Your pain tolerance must be higher than mine."

Margaret got in with him. They shivered, but together they laughed.

As they climbed the stairs outside back to the top floor, Margaret noticed a single icicle hanging off the roof. It was pathetic compared to the icicles she had gotten used to growing up in another state, sharp icicles several feet long hanging off the roof of her father's house, threatening to crash onto Margaret when she walked underneath them, returning from school. This icicle was cute in a disgusting way, like a teenager's dangling rhinestone earring. She thought of diamonds. Her understanding was that diamonds were strong, just like, ideally, the love of an engaged couple. Diamonds were strong enough to cut glass, and they lasted forever. This was why engagement rings featured diamonds. That and because they were expensive, thus proving the man's dedication to the woman. Traditionally, proving to the woman's father that the man had enough money to take care of her. Margaret thought this was a load of capitalist crap, and that it was also sexist. The ring was supposed to signal to other men that the woman was taken, but the man was not expected to wear a ring until marriage. Despite his faults, there were things Andrew had understood about Margaret that James never would.

Margaret held the door open for James at the jewelry store, waiting for him to go inside first, even though she knew he always insisted she go first. They stood there gesturing at each other for several moments while sophisticated store employees waited to greet them. Margaret averted her eyes. "Hi!" said a middle-aged woman wearing a lot of makeup and no wedding ring. "What can I help you with today?"

Margaret smiled meekly and glanced at the woman, then quickly moved her gaze to the floor. Her shoulders hunched into her body, as if she were a scared little turtle and not an adult professor of Gender Studies. James waited several seconds, as if he still expected Margaret to answer. Then he said, "engagement rings."

"Great! Follow me," said the woman.

Margaret and James sat down in some armchairs in front of a long glass case of rings. Margaret felt suddenly unprepared. She had never tried on an engagement ring, did not know how much diamonds actually cost, and did not understand the rules about which types of gold looked good on which skin "undertones."

"So," the woman said, "do you have any idea what sort of ring you're looking for?"

Margaret scanned the endless collection of rings, arranged in lines like rows of corn. "Not really."

The woman nodded. Margaret knew the woman could sense how uncomfortable she was. She feared the woman would interpret this to mean she did not love James.

The woman removed the glass lid off the case and picked up a ring. Another woman appeared behind the first, holding a tray of chocolate and nuts. "Would you like some snacks?" asked the woman. "How about something to drink?" Margaret felt as if she were in a hotel she couldn't afford, and again, the woman could tell. Margaret also wondered why they would offer chocolate to customers trying on rings. The rings must get smudged.

"No, thank you," said Margaret, as James reached for the almonds. Margaret put the ring on. She turned her face from side to side. She looked like a grandmother. She was not used to seeing any rings at all on her fingers.

The woman laughed. Margaret felt obligated to try on several more rings and to pretend to like some of them. Margaret learned that diamonds cost several thousands of dollars, even the ones that weren't that big. She communicated with her eyes to James that she wanted to leave, so they did, after the woman wrote down all the rings Margaret pretended to like, and James's phone number. Margaret knew they would not call James.

On the way home, they passed a row of houses with the Christmas lights still up. Margaret used to like Christmas, like most happy people. Now, when she saw Christmas decorations, she felt panic because she was reminded of Andrew's mangled body on the hospital bed, blood and dirt covering his broken teeth. He was hideous. Margaret had the sense he was possessed by a demon. Now, when Margaret felt the cold in winter, she thought of the head-shaped dent Andrew had made in the frosted ground beneath his mother's balcony. Margaret had told Andrew's mother she would fill the dent in with dirt; the mother didn't want to see it. The mother closed the drapes on the sliding glass door to the balcony, and didn't open them again. Margaret had put her hands in the dent and felt the cold dirt every way she could. She even put her head in the dent, imagined how that would feel, falling from so high up.

"What's wrong?" James asked.

Margaret didn't answer right away. Sometimes she had trouble forming words. James understood this problem, and was always patient with Margaret, but she could tell that this time, he needed her to answer. He knew she was upset, and he probably needed to know it wasn't his fault. He was probably worried she'd changed her mind and didn't want to marry him.

"I love you," she said, in an attempt to buy time, try to figure out what was wrong so that she could tell him. She rubbed his leg and smiled. He smiled back.

"I love you, too."

"I'm sorry," she said, "but I don't know what's wrong." She noticed that she needed to urinate, and dreaded going home, where she'd have to use the bathroom in the cold, haunted, abandoned apartment downstairs before going up to sit idly in front of the space heater like a cat.

James glanced at her sympathetically, like she was a child he was glad to take care of. He gave her this look often. Margaret had dated bad men in the past, then finally listened to her friends and pretended to value herself and find a respectful partner. Because James was not an asshole, or at least, not anymore, Margaret sometimes took this as license to stop trying and just act like a child. For this, she felt guilty.

"Margaret, if you don't want to get engaged right now, that's okay," he said. "There's no rush. The point is that we love each other. We can wait as long as you want."

She couldn't believe how nice he was to her. "No, no," she said. "I want to. I just have some things to think about. Maybe we can go to another store tomorrow."

He put his hand on hers and smiled. They drove the rest of the way in silence.

At home, James went upstairs while Margaret used the restroom in the abandoned apartment. He had offered to go with her because it was scary, but she told him she could handle it on her own. She insisted. James always wanted to be where she was. He looked a little sad to leave her, that she said she didn't need him.

It was now dark, and Margaret reluctantly turned on the main light/ceiling fan, which once again began to spin. In her mind she heard the sound of sharpening knives. She imagined sharpening icicles, diamonds. She thought for a moment about the problematic diamond industry, why someone in Africa should die just so some white American woman could have a pretty stone in her ring. She shrugged the thought off, and was surprised how little this idea bothered her. She thought of eating meat, how it secretly gave her a small, sick pleasure knowing an animal had died so she could have a meal. She thought of the slaughter, blood pouring out of a fresh throat. She wanted to hunt, like Andrew had taught her to do. She wanted to kill something. Killing was decisive, final. Andrew had joined the Marines not out of some dumb patriotism, but because he wanted to be a killer without going to prison. And he was a killer. He still sent her text messages regularly, saying nothing, saying, *It's raining hard*, saying, *I killed a deer. I ate her heart*. She took her time responding to the messages, in order to feign disinterest, when in reality she read the messages over and over until she had them memorized and could repeat them to herself in her mind.

She kept the bathroom door open as she urinated. Again, she noticed that she was bleeding. Men were carriers but they did not suffer. They took something sinister from one woman, and passed it onto the next, maybe even without noticing or caring.

Margaret heard a deep breathing. She thought of Andrew, how he had wanted to stop breathing. While he was in the hospital, he held his breath, still trying to die. He didn't know this wouldn't work. The body knocks itself unconscious, then breathes normally. The body wants to live. Andrew was bad for her, and Margaret hated him. After Andrew moved back in with Margaret after four months in the fancy mental hospital, he never washed the dishes, the laundry, or his own body. He slept until 2 pm, restlessly. He crushed Margaret's body when he rolled over in the night. Margaret was now committed to hating Andrew the same way successful spouses were committed to loving each other: she worked on the hatred every day. It gave her a small, sick pleasure to know he still loved her.

The breathing in the apartment got louder and heavier and seemed to radiate from the ceiling fan. The apartment was cold and Margaret could see her own silent breath. "You don't need to breathe anymore," Margaret said to the ghost. "You're dead." There was a soft laughter. Margaret rolled her eyes. She flushed the toilet and washed her hands. As she looked in the mirror, she again noticed that she had become thinner. She felt something like two hands, one on each of her thighs, rubbing her. She smacked her thighs and the hands stopped. She shivered, watched her breath take shape in the mirror like an icicle melting into a cloud, a diamond spreading into a stain on the air. She left the bathroom, glancing at her ass as she left, just to see what it looked like. Again, the hands rubbed her. She smacked them away. She thought of the time her father asked her if Andrew was good in bed. She told him never to ask that again, and finished cooking lunch for him. It was strange to think Margaret's father had never met James, and instead died thinking she would marry Andrew. And her mother died knowing nothing of her, not really.

Margaret entered the main room and saw that the annoying little strings that had dangled from the ceiling fan were gone. Instead there were several bones, like a rib cage had been taken apart and the bones hung up like sick ornaments. The ribs looked phallic and dripped blood onto the floor, making a sound like a leaking faucet and staining the floor red. "Good," Margaret said. "Something for the shit landlord to clean up." She spit on the blood stain, and rubbed it in with her foot. She remembered her father telling her not to spit. "Your mother wouldn't have liked that," he had said. She wished she could have heard her mother say it herself. It was not her father's fault that her mother died, but Margaret did not like that she learned how to be a woman from a man.

The laughter turned to growling, then to choking, gasping. Margaret wondered why it was so difficult for people to commit suicide. Her own body felt so fragile, like she could die at any moment in any number of ways—her veins cut open, her bones crushed by a heavy truck. Why was it so hard for Andrew to take his own life? He killed whole crowds of people just by throwing grenades, like baseballs. Easy. The ghost continued to choke, now in an obviously fake way, as if mocking something.

The door to the apartment opened. It was James. "The water's back on, sweetie," he said, standing in the doorway, not coming inside. He looked beautiful, not like a boyfriend but like a painting, like the nude on the wall. He looked sweet. He loved her, and she would love him in a committed way, working on it daily. She was done with killers. What was so bad about trying to heal?

Margaret went to James and kissed him. She pulled him inside the apartment and shut the door. She planned to have sex with him in the awful place, but quickly realized she could not. Instead, she said, "I'm bleeding again."

James took her hand and closed his eyes. "I'm sorry," he said. "I'm so sorry." He hugged her and stroked her hair. She had trouble understanding how someone could change so much. He kissed her forehead, then said, "I think you should go to the doctor again."

Margaret looked at the ceiling fan, which still dripped blood, although it was obvious James could not see that. She wanted to slap him for not seeing. She wanted to slap him for not being a killer, for being some half-assed version of a bad person, not able to fully commit even to evil.

"Why should *I* go to the doctor?" she asked. "It's your fault. You should have to go to the doctor, not me. But you don't have to worry about anything."

"I know," he said, lowering his gaze like a dog who's done something bad. "It's not fair—"

"Shut up," she said. She had to marry James. She couldn't go back to dating. She didn't want to risk giving any other men this disease; they could give it to other women. Women like her, who would probably be better off just focusing on their careers rather than trying to find husbands. Husbands had been proven for centuries not to make women happy.

"I don't want to talk about this anymore," she said. "Get outside."

"But—"

Margaret waved her hand for James to leave. "I'll be right there." James went out the door.

She switched the light and the ceiling fan off. The darkness extinguished the dangling bones and dripping blood, silenced the breathing. She locked the door behind her, sealing off that part of the house. She imagined plaster filling in the small gaps below the door, so that not even an ant could get in. She would never go back there. In her new life, she would have neither the need nor the desire for a place like that.

James stood there in the dark, waiting for her to come closer to him.

She saw an ant crawling towards the door. She squashed it with her foot.

THE MIRACULOUS
PREGNANT VIRGIN

ONCE UPON A TIME, a twelve-year old girl was tending her family's sheep in a field when the sky opened up and an angel descended. The angel was so bright and perfect that he was like a statue carved of gold, except he wasn't a statue, he moved and spoke like a living thing.

Mary was terrified. "Don't be afraid," said the angel. "I am an angel of the Lord, come to deliver a message."

Mary couldn't imagine what type of message the Lord could possibly have for her. She was just a shepherd's daughter, not anyone important like a king or a prophet.

"Mary," said the angel, "although you have not yet begun to show, you are currently *with child*." The angel pointed at Mary's belly.

Mary gasped. "But that can't be!" she said. She was a virgin, after all. Unless someone had raped her while she was asleep, there was no way she was pregnant. Had someone raped her while she was asleep?! She started to panic.

"There is more than one way to get pregnant," said the angel.

"What?" said Mary. "I only ever heard of the one."

"It's the Lord's baby that grows inside you," said the angel. "He is the Son of God, and he will be King."

"Isn't the Lord *everyone's* Father? But most babies also have a human father?"

The angel looked slightly annoyed. "Well, yes, but this case is different. There is no human father this time. It's just the Lord's baby. He is the Son of God, the messiah, the savior of mankind."

"The messiah?" said Mary. "I don't understand. I am human, but the Lord is not human. How can—"

"Everything will be fine," the angel said. "The baby will be human, but he is also a deity. You will birth him, and you will name him Jesus."

"Actually, I've already picked out names for my future children. The first was to be called William, after my father, whom I love dearly—"

"You will name him Jesus," said the angel. He fluttered his wings, then spread them. He seemed to be showing her how big they were, like a wolf baring its teeth. "The Lord is not somebody you want to piss off," the angel said. "Ever heard the story *Noah's Ark*? How about *Jonah and the Whale?*"

Mary nodded. "Well, yes. I've heard those stories." It's just a baby's name, Mary thought. The angel was making quite a threat referencing the Lord's past as a mass murderer. Mary could not imagine the Lord would slip back into serial killer mode over something so insignificant as one baby name. Mary thought perhaps the Lord would have a more cosmic view of things. But the angel's message was clear: Mary must comply, not just with this, but with everything going forward. This whole thing was going to be on the Lord's terms, that was clear. "Okay. Jesus it is," Mary said.

"Good girl," said the angel. Then he flew back into the sky, where all the angels live with the Lord and some of the people who have died (the good ones).

"What the *fuck?*" said Mary. The sun was setting. She put the sheep back in the barn and rushed back into the cottage. Her parents were preparing the evening meal of eggs, bread, and wine.

"Mother, Father," Mary said, "I've just seen an angel, and he says I'm pregnant."

"Take her to the loony bin at once," said Mary's father. "Angels don't appear to *females*."

Mary's father had already sold her to an older man named Joseph. They were not yet married, but they would be soon, and then Mary really *would* have to get pregnant.

"Mary," said her mother, "*Are* you pregnant? Oh, dear—Joseph cannot know! He'll never marry you if he finds out you've been ruined by another man—"

"But the angel said it was the Lord's baby," said Mary. "And I haven't been ruined. Nobody stuck anything up inside me, I promise—"

"Shh." Mary's mother looked her up and down as if examining a cow to determine whether or not it was ready for slaughter. The mother put her hand on Mary's stomach, closed her eyes, and began to hum. All else was silent for several moments. Then Mary's mother said, "I'm afraid it's true. You're pregnant."

"I guess you'll have to eat for two!" said Mary's father. He dished up the food, and gave Mary more eggs than usual.

"Oh, gross," said Mary. She did not like the idea of childbirth or even pregnancy. The infant was like a leech growing inside her, sucking up all her blood and the nutrients from the food she ate, and him not even asking first, and her stupid body just giving everything away to the baby for free.

"So, whose baby is it?" asked Mary's father.

"I told you!" said Mary. "The angel said it was the Lord's baby."

"Well," said the father, "there's only one way to find out."

The next morning, Mary's parents took her to the doctor, who lived in a cottage on the edge of town. "Our daughter is pregnant," said the father.

The doctor grimaced. "But she is not yet married!" he said.

The father shrugged.

"It's the Lord's baby!" said Mary.

The doctor raised his eyebrows at the father.

"I'm a virgin!" said Mary.

"We need you to check if she's a virgin," said the father.

And so the doctor had Mary lay down on a table. He lifted her dress and poked her with cold tools. She felt strange, painful sensations she'd never felt before. "Ow!" she said. The doctor took the silver tools away.

"It can't be," said the doctor.

"What?" asked Mary's mother.

"The girl is a virgin. The baby is the Lord's!" The doctor knelt down and bowed to Mary. Then he got up and kissed her hand. "You have been blessed with a great honor, Miss Mary."

"Oh, how wonderful!" said Mary's mother, beaming. Her father was beaming too.

"Hmm," said Mary. She did sort of wonder why the Lord hadn't asked her first, before magically impregnating her. Wasn't the Lord supposed to be perfect? Wouldn't it have been polite to ask first? This was all rather alarming. And perhaps the Lord could have also spoken to her directly about it, instead of sending his angel employee to deliver a message.

"This is literally the greatest honor you could have possibly brought to our family, Mary," said her father. "I am so, so proud of you." He kissed Mary's forehead.

The next evening, there was a big celebration in honor of Mary and the Lord's baby. The doctor had spread word to the town, and the town prophet backed him up. Everyone believed (or at least pretended to believe) the town prophet: it was a miracle. At the celebration there was music, dancing, and all the best foods: meat and fish and cakes. Best of all, everyone brought Mary presents. People who usually ignored Mary came to pay their respects and give her flowers, clothes, and even a few jewels. Mary had never had nice things like this before. It was the best party she had ever seen, and it was all for her. Perhaps being pregnant with the Lord's baby isn't so bad after all, Mary thought. I could get used to this lifestyle. It's sort of like being married to the king.

Then Joseph appeared next to her, and she remembered that her father had already sold her to Joseph, that she actually had to marry someone who was *not* a king. Suddenly Mary felt as if Joseph was not good enough for her. She had been chosen by the *Lord* to carry his son. He could have magically impregnated any girl on Earth without asking first, but he chose Mary. She must be very special indeed. Joseph was nothing but a carpenter.

"Mary," Joseph said. Joseph was thirty years old, tall and thin with a full beard. He was not bad-looking, but Mary was not sexually attracted to him. Mary was not exactly sexually attracted to anyone. Sometimes she imagined kissing boys, but not having sex with them. Sex seemed vulgar, and like it would hurt. She had seen the doctor's tools, which were quite small. But they had still hurt, and made her bleed. Imagine what a man could do.

"Joseph," said Mary. She had not yet spoken to him, not since her encounter with the angel. Mary's father had explained everything to Joseph, though, and he'd reported to Mary that Joseph took it all fine. "Joseph, I just want you to know—"

"Shh," he said, putting a finger up to Mary's lips. "I know, Mary. I believe you. I mean, I didn't at first. I was planning to quietly break things off between us, but then an angel appeared in my dream and told me not to be afraid to *take* you, because it is the Lord's baby."

Mary frowned.

"I know you'd never betray me," Joseph said. "You're a good girl, Mary. The Lord recognized that, and blessed you with this gift. Blessed *us* with this gift. I will stand by you and help you raise the child as if he were my own." Joseph held his head high. "I've always wanted to be a father," he said.

"But you're not the father," said Mary. She swept her arm around in a circle to show many people were at the celebration. "That's kind of what this whole thing is about."

"Well, yes, but—I just meant that I'm happy for you, and I want you to know that I'm not going to leave you."

"You can be like the stepfather, I guess," said Mary. "If it's okay with the Lord. The angel made it very clear that this is all going to be on the Lord's terms."

Joseph nodded. "I'm sure it will be okay." He squeezed Mary's hand. "I love you, Mary," he said. He had never said this to her before. She didn't know what to do.

"Thank you, Joseph," she said.

Joseph nodded. Then, mercifully, he walked away to talk to some other men.

That night as she lay in bed, Mary began to have disturbing thoughts about the baby and his father. If God was *everyone's* Father, then he was Mary's Father, too. It was gross for fathers to impregnate daughters. Although it had happened many times before, Mary didn't like it. The thought of being impregnated by her own human father was more than Mary could bear. It made her want to vomit and then die. Also, would this make Jesus her brother as well as her son?

A few months went by like normal. Mary helped her family with the sheep and other animals. She took walks along her little stream in the woods. She addressed her prayers to the father of her child. She went to visit her cousin, who was also pregnant. Her belly began slowly to grow, so that now she actually looked pregnant. Mary examined herself in her mother's mirror. She frowned. This wasn't how a pregnant woman was supposed to look. Where were her breasts? Mary had hardly developed any breasts at all so far, not like the girls of sixteen or seventeen. It was true her breasts had swelled slightly since the pregnancy, but still, they were quite small. Mary wondered how they could possibly hold enough milk to feed the baby. You could fit maybe a tablespoon in each, but that was hardly anything! She supposed the Lord would help her out, somehow. The Lord often allowed regular babies to die, but Mary was sure he wouldn't let that happen to the *messiah*, the boy who was supposed to save all mankind.

One morning at home, Mary woke with a start. It was very early, still dark outside, and she'd heard a loud crashing sound. Mary jumped out of bed, clutched her nightgown tight against her body. She put her ear against her bedroom door. Had someone broken in? She looked around for a weapon, and found only a heavy candlestick. She grabbed it and slowly opened her bedroom door.

Mary didn't see anyone there, but she did see that the house was completely torn apart. The table and chairs had been broken with an axe. The walls had been slashed, too. The floor was littered with broken glass from jars and dishes. Food was smeared on the walls and the floor. The door to outside was wide open.

"Mother! Father!" Mary called. She ran to their bedroom door and pounded on it. They came out.

"What is it?" her mother asked. "What happened?"

Mary showed them the damage. "Oh, Lord," said her father.

"Yes," Mary said. "Oh, Lord."

They looked around. Nothing had actually been stolen— whoever broke in had just wanted to trash things, to cause damage. They went outside to look at the house from a different perspective. Someone had taken an axe to the outside, too. It looked as if a hurricane had attacked just this one house. Across the front door in red paint, the words:

WATCH OUT, SLUT!

Mary's mother sighed, then calmly said, "So they've finally come. The unbelievers."

"What?" said Mary.

"I was wondering when this would happen."

Mary stared at her mother. "Well, you seem quite unsurprised!"

"Of course I'm not surprised, honey," her mother said. "I mean, are *you* surprised? Really? Did you think everyone was just going to believe you that it's the Lord's baby you're carrying?"

"Well, kind of, yeah," said Mary. "Because it *is* the Lord's baby. Plus, everyone seemed to believe me when we had that celebration! People brought me *presents*. I never get presents normally."

"Well," said her mother, "yes, I can see how that would be confusing to someone like you. But, I have to break it to you: not everyone believes you. Not even back then, they didn't. But enough of them did that those who didn't had to pretend they did. You know what I mean? Now enough time has passed for people to think it over a bit. And really, it just doesn't make sense. Why would the Lord choose *you* to carry his magic messiah child? You're just a shepherd's daughter. No offense, I love you more than anything, honey, it's just that to someone like the Lord, you can't possibly be that impressive. Why wouldn't he choose some sort of princess or queen? Or at least someone glamorous, someone highly valued for her beauty? Perhaps someone who has already borne children, to be sure she could handle it, without dying? Perhaps someone a bit..." Mary's mother again looked her up and down as if assessing whether or not a cow was ready for slaughter. "Perhaps someone a bit more mature, particularly in the chest and hips departments."

"Mom!" Mary said.

"Sorry," said Mary's mother.

Mary began to cry. "It's okay," Mary said to her mother. "You're right. It doesn't make sense. Why would the Lord pick *me?* I'm nobody! I'm nothing."

Mary's mother put her arms around Mary and kissed the top of her head. "Oh, sweetie," she said. "My darling girl. My sweet princess." Her mother rubbed her hand over Mary's belly, and began to hum the tune of a lullaby.

"Well," said Mary's father to no one in particular, for he was not looking at the women and not speaking very loud at all, "I guess I'll go get my toolbox."

Joseph helped Mary's father rebuild those parts of the house that could be rebuilt. Some things were simply beyond repair, and would have to be replaced entirely, little by little, as they did not have enough money to cover everything at once.

"Is there even any point?" Mary asked. "Won't the unbelievers just come back, and destroy everything all over again?"

"It's possible," said Joseph. "But we have to try. You're worth it."

"That's what I like to hear!" said Mary's father. He clapped Joseph on the back. "Mary, this man will make a good husband, and a good father to Jesus."

Joseph beamed.

"Although, of course, technically you aren't his father," said Mary's father.

"True," said Mary. "He's not."

Joseph wiped the smile off his face, then went back to rebuilding things.

Mary supposed she should be a little more grateful for Joseph. After all, he had believed her about the baby and not rejected or threatened her. And he was nice, much nicer than a lot of other men in town.

Mary decided to go on a walk to clear her head. "I'm fine," she said to Joseph, her father, and her mother, when they asked where she was going and why. "I just want to clear my head."

"Do you want one of us to come with you?" asked Joseph.

"No, thank you," Mary said.

Joseph nodded. He tried to smile but Mary could see the hurt in his eyes. She must try to be nicer to Joseph. He was a good man. He wanted to help her raise the baby as if it were his own. A lot of men wouldn't be able to handle that, knowing the baby wasn't theirs. A lot of men would send the baby away. Mary didn't want to send the baby away. She had grown quite attached to him at this point. She didn't know whether or not she'd be able to let him out, when the time came. He was part of her body. He was just a part of her body. It was like nothing had changed at all, and yet everything had changed. People said she was two now instead of one. Mary and Jesus, both contained inside Mary. How could one life live inside another?

"You really shouldn't go out alone," said her father. "Not after what they wrote."

Mary and Joseph walked to her little stream, not speaking. Joseph held Mary's hand to help her sit down on a large rock. Together they watched the water in the stream flow along. They listened to the water knock against the pebbles. They listened to the hum of dragonflies. Suddenly Mary felt her face move itself toward Joseph's, she felt her lips kiss him on the mouth and she felt him kiss her back, feeling the two drink each other in like water in a parched desert.

Mary moved off of Joseph and looked back at the stream. "He's just part of my body," she said.

"Pregnancy is a miracle," said Joseph. "You have the power to give life."

"I don't want this," Mary said.

"You don't want what?"

"This is all wrong. I had already planned things out. I wanted to name my first male child William, after my father, because I love my father, you know? Of course, if you wanted to name him after *your* father, I would be open to that, just as long as we had an additional male child so we could name one William. And I also planned to get pregnant *after* getting married. This isn't fair. I followed the rules and stayed a virgin, and for what? To get impregnated against my will, with no choice at all in the matter, and people ruined our house and broke all our stuff and I never did anything to deserve that!"

Joseph put his hand on hers, signaling that he wanted, needed her to stop talking. "Mary, you shouldn't say such things. The Lord has given you a very important job. You should be honored! I need you to be good, Mary. I need you to be a good girl."

"I'm your wife," said Mary.

"Yes," said Joseph. "I'm very happy about that, my sweet Mary."

"I'm not a good girl," she said. "I'm a woman."

Joseph squinted his eyes at her and scrunched up his face. He looked very skeptical indeed.

"I'm going to be a mother, Joseph," she said.

"Well, yes, I suppose you are," he said.

Mary looked at the trees, at the ends of their branches where the wood was thin and sharp. She had heard about a procedure certain doctors could perform, witch doctors, a procedure involving a sharp object inserted into a woman which could rid her of her trouble...Perhaps Mary could find someone to do this for her.

The sky opened up like an earthquake, and the golden angel descended from the world above the clouds.

"You must not think of such things, Mary," said the angel.

"Speak of the devil," Mary replied.

The angel screamed, then made a cross out of his hands. He looked around frantically, but when he saw there was no devil around, he relaxed.

Mary looked over at Joseph. He was apparently watching the stream, unaware of the angel. "Joseph?" Mary said. He didn't answer. She moved her hand in front of his face, but he didn't react.

"He can't see me," said the angel. "He isn't aware of any of this. He won't remember it."

"Well, why not?" Mary asked. "You appeared to him in a dream, so why not now?"

"Actually, I didn't appear to Joseph in a dream," said the angel. "That was just...a dream Joseph had, I guess. That was just a coincidence."

"Well, maybe you could appear to him now. Not just him, actually, but the whole town, and maybe you could tell them the truth? That would sure make things a lot easier for me and my family. You know, someone just trashed our house. They broke a bunch of our stuff, and we can't afford to fix it all. Plus, they threatened me and called me a slut."

"Don't say 'slut,'" said the angel.

"But—"

"Don't say it."

"But you just said it."

"Mary, haven't you ever heard the phrase, 'Do as I say, not as I do'? This is one of those situations where that phrase applies. I am like one of the king's officers: I'm allowed to break the rules in order to make sure that others don't break the rules. As for your question about me telling the villagers the truth, you already know I can't do that. Angels can't just talk to everyone. Then everyone would *know* that we're real. Then there would be no test of faith. The Lord wants people to accept him without being given a reason to accept him. That's how he determines whether or not someone gets into Heaven."

"About that," said Mary. "Why did the Lord send you to tell me I was pregnant? Why couldn't he speak to me himself?"

"He's very busy," said the angel.

"Well, yes, but this is his child we're talking about."

"We are all children of the Lord," said the angel. "Do you think he has time to visit every girl who gets herself pregnant?"

"I didn't get myself pregnant," Mary said. "I never agreed to this. You simply informed me. Also, you said this child was special, the messiah, savior of all mankind."

The angel sighed. "Look, Mary, I don't make the rules, okay? I just do what the Lord tells me to do, *anything* he tells me to do. He does not like to be questioned, so I suggest you adjust your attitude. Have you ever heard the story of Abraham and Isaac? The Lord does not like to be questioned."

"I want out," Mary said. "I want you to take this baby away. Why don't you just put the messiah inside of a different girl? Like, maybe someone who is already married, so that nobody judges her? Maybe someone who actually *wants* to have a child right now?!" Mary was getting worked up. The more she thought about it, and the longer she looked at the angel's stupid perfect face, the angrier she got.

"Now, Mary," said the angel, "it seems you have become a bit emotional in your state. This happens sometimes to pregnant girls. I'm going to forgive you for the things you said. I know you didn't mean them. The Lord knows exactly what he's doing. Whatever his reasons for choosing you specifically to carry his child, which, believe me, I do not know what those reasons are, I don't know what he could possibly see in you, but the point is that he did choose you and he knows best."

"You're not going to take the baby away from me," Mary said. "You don't care about me at all."

"Of course I care about you, Mary!" said the angel. "I just don't care what you *think*, or what you *want*."

Mary stood up and reached out her arm to touch the angel. She felt nothing. "You're not real," she said. "None of this is real. Joseph can't see you because you're not real. I must be crazy. I've been driven crazy. Oh, God, whose baby am I carrying?" Mary began to sob.

"Mary," said the angel, "you must not pursue this line of thinking. This is the Lord's baby."

She said, "What happens if I get rid of it myself?"

The angel shuddered. "Mary, you mustn't say such things."

"But what would happen?"

The angel looked at the ground. "You know what would happen, Mary." He patted her head. "Cheer up, sweet girl. Everything is going to be okay." He flew away.

The sun was now setting. Joseph snapped out of his trance. Mary said, with a quiet sadness, "We should go back now, Joseph. But thank you for coming here with me."

"Of course, my darling," he said. "I'd do anything for you."

A few more months went by and soon it was time to pay taxes, and also a threat came in from another village. Mary and Joseph had to ride on a donkey to a faraway town even though Mary was so pregnant she was sure the baby would just fall out of her any day now. The journey was miserable. It took fourteen hours, and Mary had to stop and pee in the bushes about every thirty minutes.

When they got to the town, it was late. They'd have to spend the night and pay taxes the next day. The couple knocked on the door of every hotel in the whole town. No place had any room. They knocked on the doors of houses, offering money in exchange for shelter. No one had any room. It was cold and dark. Finally, the couple came to the last house in town. "I don't have any room in the house," said an old man, "but you can sleep in the stable with the animals."

"Hmph," said Mary. A few months ago, she'd been showered with wonderful gifts, candy and gems, and now she was supposed to sleep on a bed of hay with some piglets?

"Oh, Mary," Joseph said. "It will be okay. We have each other!" He took the blanket out of their bag and wrapped Mary in it. He fluffed the hay and lay her down on it. "My sweet Mary," he said.

"Wait a second," Mary said. She winced and put her hand on her stomach. Something burst inside her and she was wet. She looked down and saw the wetness. "Joseph," she said.

"Oh, Lord," said Joseph. He jumped up. "Wait here, Mary. I'll find someone to help us. Don't worry, my love! I'll be back!" Joseph rushed off.

Mary exhaled audibly. "Come back quick!" she tried to say, but her voice was so quiet she could barely even hear herself, so there was no way Joseph heard her.

The sky opened up and the golden angel descended. Mary was breathing in and out frantically. Her body was about to explode, rip in half, open up like the sky just did. Would she survive the childbirth? Would Joseph find help in time? Mary knew the Lord would protect the baby, but she didn't know whether he would spare *her* life as well.

"Oh, relax," said the angel. "Don't be so dramatic. The Lord will let you live. He is grateful to you for your service, Mary."

Mary glared at him. She hated that angel, with his stupid golden skin and perfect symmetrical features. Mary felt herself begin to open. It was excruciating. "Ow!" she screamed. She arched her body and threw her head back. "Ow!"

"You need to push," said the angel.

"No, thanks," said Mary. She wanted to hold it in. If she let it go, she'd rip in half, she knew it. She'd die.

"Push," said the angel.

"You're trying to trick me," she said. "You don't care about me. All you care about is this baby. Once he's born, you'll have no more use for me. You'll forget me."

"Oh, Mary," said the angel. "The Catholics won't forget you. Thousands of years from now, they'll still put your face on candles they light while making wishes. The Protestants will sort of forget about you, though, I guess that's true. Actually, what's interesting is, there will be more about you in the Quran than the Bible. The Quran will have a whole chapter about you."

"What?" said Mary.

"Don't worry about it," he said. "Just push!"

Mary closed her eyes and let out a scream. Into that scream she put all of her anger at the angel, at the Lord, at the people who ruined her house and called her a slut, at her father for selling her to Joseph, at Jesus for hurting her so much right now with his gigantic, awkwardly-shaped body forcing itself through a tiny tunnel. At herself for being so weak.

"Just get it out of me!" she screamed. She pushed as hard as she possibly could, and then she pushed harder.

"Good girl," said the angel.

Mary roared.

When Mary came to, she saw Joseph hovering over her, holding a baby. Beside him was another man, who Mary supposed was a doctor. The baby was quiet.

"She's awake!" said Joseph. "Mary, do you want to hold him?"

Mary shifted herself up a bit. She could feel a wet mess beneath her, inside her, on top of her. Everywhere, a mess of blood and shit and other fluids and snake cords and pieces of slimy flesh to be tossed away, garbage. She took the baby from Joseph and looked into his eyes. She wondered if the baby had special abilities, being a deity and all. She looked around for the golden angel, but he was gone now. The baby's eyes looked very intelligent, like he was an adult person inside an infant's body, like he could already read and hear and understand human language. It freaked her out. She felt the baby was trying to deceive her. "I'm your *mother*," she said to the baby. "Don't look at me like that."

"Haha?" said Joseph.

Mary glared at Joseph, then handed the baby back. She realized she was a very strict, harsh mother. She said, "I'm going back to sleep now," and closed her eyes. No one bothered her the rest of the night.

Mary, Joseph, and Jesus had to stay in the stable for a few days, because Mary was not well enough to travel.

"I'm never going to have another baby," Mary said, nursing Jesus in the stable.

"Mary!" said Joseph. "You mustn't say such things."

"It hurts so horribly, Joseph," she said. "You could never understand."

Joseph sighed. "Oh, Mary," he said. "I'm sorry it hurts. But you know we have to have children! That's what married people do."

"But I don't think I can survive another one," she said. "The angel protected me this time, but they don't need me anymore. I've served my purpose. The Lord has already written the story of Jesus, a plan for how he's going to save all of mankind. This is where I exit the story. Other people pretty much take the reins from here on out."

"What do you mean?" Joseph asked.

"I mean I never asked for any of this," said Mary.

Joseph's eyes filled with hurt. Mary really must try to be nicer to Joseph. But it was true, she hadn't asked for any of this, and she didn't *want* any of it. She was almost thirteen now. It was time for her to take her life into her own hands.

Just then, three magnificent men arrived on camels. They had long, silver beards, wore purple and gold robes, and jeweled crowns glittered on their heads. "We followed the Star of Bethlehem," said the men. "We have come to see the King."

Joseph bowed to the men, then picked up the baby Jesus and showed him off. The men oohed and aahed. "We've brought gifts," said the magnificent men. They handed Joseph some gold, plus some pointless herbs or something. Mary stayed quiet this whole time, hoping the men would leave soon.

Later, the men were gone and the baby was asleep. Everything was dark and peaceful. Donkeys and piglets munched quietly on pieces of hay. "Tomorrow we can journey back, I think," said Joseph.

"Yes," said Mary. "I think I'll be well enough in the morning."

"Get a good night's rest," said Joseph.

"You too," said Mary. They both shut their eyes.

Mary waited in darkness for a very long time, turning things over in her mind. When she was as sure as she'd ever be that both Joseph and the baby were asleep, she gently stood up. She went to their bags. She took everything out of both, then put all her things in one. She took half the gold the fancy men had brought, and left the other half for Joseph. It was a lot of gold. She felt very lucky, holding it in her hands. She put the gold safely away in her bag. She grabbed an axe from the wall. She'd need a weapon, traveling alone. Yes, she was abandoning a helpless baby, but he was with Joseph, and Joseph could raise the baby better than Mary could.

She still felt like a child herself. Perhaps Joseph would find himself a different wife to help him. She'd leave now on the donkey she and Joseph rode in on. She'd reach her parents before Joseph possibly could. She'd tell them that she loves them, but she must leave, she must go to another town and start over. "You can come with me if you want," she'd say to her parents. "In fact, I'd prefer it if you did come with me. We're not safe here. Our lives will never be the same. I never asked for any of this. Will you come with me?" And maybe her parents would say yes, or maybe they'd say no because they're old and they've lived in that village their whole lives and they've never known anything else and that's always been okay with them, and they're too tired to try anything else now, they're ready to settle in and die. Maybe Mary would have to go on her own. She'd use the gold to get a place to stay, and she'd find a job helping some people herd their sheep, and make clothing out of the sheep's hair, make houses and beds and coffins out of sheep's hair, so they can wrap up their lives in sheep's clothing, make them look like something they're not.

THE HOUSE

CARA'S MOTHER ALWAYS MAKES Cara do things that should get her in trouble—spit off bridges, sneak into the Employees Only closet, feed old bread to animals at the zoo. "Don't tell your father," she says, and Cara doesn't, because she doesn't want to get in trouble. Cara's mother is an actress at the theater and she steals costumes and fake fruit from the prop closet. She says you're not guilty if you don't get caught. But when Cara's father comes home from the office and asks about the new centerpiece, her mother says they were having a sale at the craft store. Then she makes a face at Cara like, "Shh...our little secret!"

But I don't want it to be our little secret, Cara thinks, *because it's not fun.* At school Cara does everything right: she makes a cubicle out of her folders during spelling tests, she doesn't cut in the lunch line, she gets stickers on all her assignments. She has nightmares where she's at school, but she can't find her shoes. It's against the rules not to wear your shoes.

Cara's mother loves to explore the new, empty houses being built nearby. She takes Cara on walks after dinner, once all the construction workers have gone home. She makes Cara wander through the half-built rooms, rooms that will soon hold babies' toys and Thanksgiving dinners, but are, for now, drafty brown boxes. The stairs feel unstable.

Her mother never listens when Cara doesn't want to do something. She always says, "Calm down, honey. You're just like your father. Everything is fine. Have a little fun!" But it's not fun. It is never fun. Cara likes Checkers and math. Cara's father likes math, too; he says he uses it at work. Her mother thinks math is boring. She likes costume parties, dancing, and wine.

Today on their afternoon walk, Cara and her mother come to a house that doesn't look half-built. The walls are sealed together and the house is painted, with a garden and a car in the driveway. In the half-built houses, you can walk right through the empty frames, and there are certainly no gardens or cars. Cara's mother wants to go inside this house anyway.

"Mom, this is someone's house. Someone lives here," Cara says.

"Don't be silly," her mother says, dismissing this comment with a wave of her hand, walking up the driveway and leaving Cara behind.

"Mom, we can't go inside," Cara calls. "That's not allowed. Can we please go home?"

Cara's mother looks at her. "Sweetie, I don't know what you're talking about," she says, opening the door.

Cara rushes after to try and stop her, but her mother waltzes right in, opening her arms and spinning around in the space, thinking up a story of the house's future inhabitants like she always does. "A mom and a dad and a girl and a cat!" she says, running her hands along the walls, on which, Cara sees, pictures hang. Inside the house, it is warm.

"Mom, I'm telling you, somebody lives here. Just look at the pictures!"

Cara's mother hums as she opens all the cupboards, as if looking for something to cook.

Cara tries not to touch anything herself; she heard the police can catch criminals with their fingerprints. "Mom, we've got to leave before someone calls the police."

Cara's mother acts like she cannot hear Cara's words. She keeps humming and spinning, wiping her fingerprints all over the walls and stomping loudly on the floor. *This is hopeless*, Cara thinks. She wants to leave, but she's not sure of the way back, and it's dangerous to walk around alone in the evening. Waiting for this to end could take forever, plus the residents could come home any minute. Or come downstairs.

Cara takes one last glance at her mother, who is now chopping potatoes on the kitchen's island, not even using a cutting board. "Potato salad tomorrow!" her mother says, seemingly to herself. *Hopeless*, Cara thinks again. Cara decides the only thing to do is go upstairs and see if anyone's home. She could at least explain that none of this is her fault.

"Hello?" she calls up the stairs, but no answer. "Is anyone home? I'm not a robber, I'm just a little girl." She grips the banister and walks slowly up the stairs.

There is a long hallway with four doorways, three on the left and one on the right. The door on the right is closed, which makes Cara think it is a bathroom. She does not want to open that door. Cara cranes her head through one doorway on the left, a bedroom, but no one is inside. No one behind the second bedroom door either. And no one behind the third, but Cara goes inside the room anyway, because it is the last one.

There is hardly anything in the room. Just some shelves holding books that must weigh a million pounds each, like her father's, plus a desk and a chair. On the desk is a gold watch and a computer. Cara loves watches. Her father collects them, and one time he took the back off of one and showed her all the gears clicking inside to keep time, like a tiny mechanical heartbeat, the heartbeat of a robot.

Cara is overcome with the urge to take the back off this watch, but she mustn't, because this is someone else's house, and besides, she doesn't know where the tools are. She would also like to have the watch for herself, but she would never steal. Instead, she moves her hand as close as possible to the watch without touching it, and then her ear, and then her nose.

"Cara!" someone says behind her, and she jumps. She looks back and sees her father. "Dad!" she says. Never has she been so relieved.

"Cara, what are you doing in here? Were you about to steal my watch?"

"I didn't even touch it!" Cara says. Then she realizes he said, *my watch.* "And it's not yours!"

Cara's father takes off his glasses, closes his eyes and rubs his temples with his hands. "Oh, Cara," he says, sounding tired. "We've been over this so many times."

Cara's mother appears behind her father. "What's wrong?" she asks, kissing his cheek. When he doesn't answer, her eyes move to Cara, and then to the watch.

"Oh, Cara, not again," she says. She looks back at Cara's father, and he nods.

"Again," he says. "Why don't you go downstairs and finish that new potato salad recipe for tomorrow. I'll talk to Cara."

"But Mom can't possibly follow a recipe!" says Cara. "She doesn't like anything with rules! She makes me break into houses, she steals from the theater, she leaves restaurants without paying..." Cara is breathing very hard and she feels her face getting hot. "She cheats when we play Checkers and she called my teacher a dimwit!"

Cara's mother shoots her a hateful glare before spinning out of the room.

"Cara," her father says, putting his glasses back on and looking her straight in the eyes, "you're really a pain in the neck."

DOCTOR'S OFFICE PAPERWORK

New Patient Intake Form

Instructions: Please answer the questions, then return this form to Sally, the woman at the desk.

Name:
My Japanese great-grandmother immigrated to California. She shed her birth name, Kino, and replaced it with Mary. She married a white American Navy man. He went off to fight in World War II, while Mary and her two young children were taken to a Japanese Internment Camp.

Now, my middle name is Mary, not Kino. I never met this woman—she died before I was born. Nobody thinks "Japanese great-grandmother" when they hear "Mary." They think "mother of Jesus" and also "Virgin." Don't even get me started on the Virgin Mary.

Caitlin, my first name, is the Irish form of Catherine, which means Purity. So far, it's looking like I'm a double virgin.

Vance, my English last name, means "dweller of bog" or "one who lives near the marshland."

As far as I know, I am not Irish or English. I don't know

"what" all I am, besides Japanese and German. My family did not keep records. Some of them never asked their parents what they "were," and then they died. Others were so crazy that I didn't know whether or not to trust what they claimed. "You're related to the Last Samurai," my grandma used to say. Why is Tom Cruise in that movie? "You're related to a Blackfoot princess," my grandma used to say, while we watched Disney's *Pocahontas*. "And a Welsh princess, too." Once I save $200 I will get 23andMe, maybe. But it doesn't seem very legit.

Caitlin Mary Vance: or, "Bog-Dwelling, Double-Virgin Mother of a Non-Japanese Male Deity."

Birthday:

I tend to sleep my birthdays away.

I identify with SOME of the qualities associated with my astrological sign: I am curious, adaptable, and nervous. I am inconsistent, indecisive, restless. Cerebral, gentle, and affectionate. I contain two personalities in one. I forever seek a missing other half that in fact does not exist. I make too many wishes.

However, I do not feel like the life of the party. Aren't Geminis supposed to be the life of the party?

Contact Information:

You can find me reading in the pink chair with high walls like a womb.

Emergency Contact Information:

While in the midst of an emergency, I tend not to answer the phone.

Please list any health problems that you and/or members of your blood family have:

Brain cancer, lung cancer, COPD, heart disease, stroke, clinical depression, OCD, bipolar disorder, seizures, body dysmorphia, PTSD, insomnia, alcoholism, drug addiction, agoraphobia.

What do you eat for breakfast?

Coffee. Powdered, chocolate-flavored vitamins mixed with soymilk. Two yellow pills, one pink, half of a white.

How much do you drink?

I kind of hate alcohol, but I drink beers at poetry readings because it seems weird not to. They are always holding poetry readings at bars. I feel I always have to pay for the space I take up.

Do you smoke or use other tobacco products?

Years ago on the first day of school, the poetry teacher asked each student what we loved most. My real answer was humiliating. I made something up instead. My girlfriend at the time said "reading."

Recently I went to a beautiful wedding on a beach. The next day I got a respiratory infection and coughed my way into a lost voice. I slept away the next two weeks. Never have I felt so useless. Never have I been so aware that my body is aging, and that part of aging is sickness.

I no longer enjoy cigarettes, because of their association with coughing. I don't even smoke them when I'm drunk. Then again, I never get drunk anymore. My uncle died a few days ago. He hadn't been able to breathe for a long time. He had a breathing machine like Darth Vader. Perhaps my favorite word from academia is post-human.

Are you currently pregnant?

No. I wish, but I need to procure money first and I don't know how to do that. Plus, several people have suggested that I'm too crazy to have a child. The child will be crazy, too, they fear.

Have you ever been pregnant?

No.

Would you like to speak to someone about birth control today?

Oh, yes—Congress, the Supreme Court, the White House, extremist religious groups, medical researchers, and all the men who have sex with women.

When was the date of your last menstrual period?

I couldn't be more proud to say that I'm finally synced up with the moon. When she is full and bright, I am bleeding.

Can you start with 100, then subtract seven over and over and tell me what number you end up with?

No, thanks. You can just mark me down as impaired, or whatever.

Do you have any plans to carry out suicide or murder?

Certainly not. I would never kill myself unless I *knew* I would otherwise face a worse death. For instance, if someone was about to chop me into pieces and then eat the pieces in front of me (and they'd eat my eyes last), and I saw a gun within reach but the gun was enchanted so that I couldn't use it to shoot the murderer, I could only use it to shoot myself, and there was no possibility of escaping the scenario, I'd shoot myself in the head because I know exactly the right way to do it so you actually die, you don't just cause yourself a lot of pain and wake up later in a hospital bed with tubes in all your orifices, and I don't like that I know the best way to successfully die but I do, someone told it to me. I won't be the one to tell it to you, doctor, nurse, Sally, or whoever is reading this form. But it would be pretty easy to look up, if you're curious.

More realistically, though, say I live to old age and then I'm diagnosed with some terminal, terrible illness like COPD. Rather than just letting the suffering get worse and worse until I shrivel into a raisin and die alone in a hospital while my future grown children are out for a few minutes sitting in line at a Chick-fil-A drive-thru, I might prefer, upon being diagnosed with some shitty illness, to just go to a wonderful beach with all my friends and family (the ones who are still alive) and all their dogs. We could have a potluck party and a poetry reading on the beach, perhaps take some MDMA, light tiki torches, bounce in a bouncy castle, then everyone would go around in a circle and say their favorite things about me. Then I'd take whatever kind of poison is closest to painless, and float out to sea on a little raft clutching a bouquet of bleeding hearts, my favorite flower, and mermaids could eat my corpse.

Or perhaps I'd also kill myself if I knew I were about to face something even worse than death—whatever death even is. These days they say God's not real, therefore death is only oblivion, or nothing, or darkness.

I would never kill someone else unless it was in defense of someone I loved or probably even self-defense, or in defense of the good of the world...I hope I wouldn't get all French Revolution though. I really do wonder how the world may have been differ-ent if the damn French Revolution people had just been a little less sadistic, raping both living people and corpses, chopping off the head of Marie Antoinette's best friend, then parading it on a stick outside Marie Antoinette's window. A murderer on one of those Netflix documentary series about murderers describes "not being able to" kill his friend, but then "stepping past the part [of himself] that wouldn't let [him] do it."

Is the thing preventing us from killing just some invisible wall you can simply *step through?*

Have you ever started a fire?

In Nick's backyard one summer, near a pile of dry fallen leaves, we held a long lighter in front of a Super Soaker filled with gasoline we took from his dad's garage stash. That was one incident in our year of pyromania. We, at least I, never hoped for any real damage, it's just that it was summer—school was out, my mother was at work, my sister was locked in the basement, doing whatever she did all day on the internet. I was lonely, too old to find friends in the stuffed rabbit Daisy or the dinosaur Mary. I've always had an inexplicable aversion to technology. This makes me wonder if I'm less evolved than other people. I was too young for drugs and too young for sex. Fire was about right for my age.

What kind of insurance do you have?

The cheapest option on the Obamacare website.

What is the meaning of this statement? "Those who live in glass houses should not throw stones."

I've never heard this statement in my life. I'll suppose it means: being self-destructive does not make you cool.

Please sign your name in the space below, then kindly return this form to Sally. Thank you.

_____   _____

I CAN TELL WHAT'S REAL AND WHAT'S PRETEND

I can tell what's real and what's pretend, not like the people in the mind hospital with Mom. She's in the hospital because when nobody was watching, she went into the garage and tried to cut me out of her belly with a knife. Well joke's on her because I wasn't in her belly, I was already born just fine ten years ago. So instead of cutting me out, all she did was twist the knife deep into herself until she scraped her organs and got blood all over the garage floor like the oil from Grandpa's car. Grandma found Mom half-dead in the garage, then a screaming ambulance took her away. Probably the blood inside Mom shines silver now like the knife's blade.

This is not the first time Mom has tried to cut me out of her belly. She just goes crazy sometimes, always in spring or summer. When she's not crazy, she's quiet and still like a hibernating bear. In winter, blizzards come. Sharp icicles bigger than me hang off roofs and she doesn't even look up. Then the snow starts to melt. She's like a cuckoo clock, quiet for a long time and then BANG, crazy, over and over in a circle. Grandma, Grandpa and I hide all the knives and try to watch Mom closely like babysitters, but we can't watch all the time. We have lives and need to sleep. A social worker comes to visit Mom once a week when she's home. Social workers are like guardian angels who watch over sick people, but they're humans, so they make mistakes. Mom found a way to get the knife anyway and pull the same stunt. I don't know why she wants to cut me out of her.

The mind hospital is in the basement of the body hospital, even though in real life the mind is like the top floor of the body. Grandma and I take the elevator down there every night from 6-7, visiting hours. Grandma is always too tired for stairs. She's not that old for a grandma, only forty-eight. She had Mom when she was twenty-four, and Mom had me when she was sixteen. We have always lived with Grandma and Grandpa. I do not have a dad.

The mind hospital is the saddest, darkest, coldest part of the building—a maze of grey hallways with no windows. There's metal equipment everywhere, and nurses in blue outfits carry paper cups full of pills. The ceilings are too low, which makes everyone look strange, the wrong height. The ceilings make me worry I'm about to be crushed, like the flowers I put between pages of the dictionary. The hospital people try to fix the darkness down here by putting in extra-bright lights, but it doesn't fix the dark in a nice way. The lights feel fake, not like moons or candles.

The two ladies at the front desk check all visitors for sharp objects and cords. Nothing dangerous is allowed in here. Lots of the patients are like Mom, trying to cut their own bodies up. Once, a visitor had a makeup mirror in her purse and a patient took it, smashed it, and used the broken glass to cut her vein open. No more makeup mirrors allowed now.

"Hello, Anna," says Elaine, one of the smiling ladies at the front desk. "Nice to see you again." She knows my name because I've been here every day this week, plus I've been here basically every year of my life, like a tradition. The ladies at the front desk like me, and so do most of the patients. That's because I am a child. Everyone here is sad, but most adults are happy for at least one little second when they see a nice or cute child. In general, I get a lot more attention than Grandma.

"Hello, Miss Elaine," I say, and curtsy like Shirley Temple.

She thinks this is cute, so I do it every time I come here. She puts her hand over her heart and says "Anna, you are too sweet! You just made my day."

Mom can only stay here three weeks per year. That's because of insurance, which is something related to money. Adults won't explain it to me because it's too complicated. Adults keep secrets from me all the time, but I'm smarter than they think. Grandma says maybe someday we can get a different insurance and/or more money, so that Mom can go to a better hospital, a long-term one. This hospital helps like a Band-Aid, but Mom just keeps falling over and scraping her knee again. Grandma doesn't know if Mom will get worse. We need more money in general.

"Let's go to Mom's room," says Grandma. She calls her "Mom" when she's talking to me, because she thinks if she calls her by her real name I won't understand what's going on.

I blow a kiss to Miss Elaine. She blows one back.

Everybody gets a roommate here. Inside each room, there are two beds, two armchairs, and two nightstands with drawers. They put a blue curtain in between one person's half of the room and the other, like they're trying to keep the sun from shining through a window. But there are no windows here, so really they're trying to keep one person from shining too much on the other.

"Hi, Anna," says Ruth, Mom's roommate, who is sitting on her bed reading a magazine with a famous person on the cover. The blue curtain is open, because Ruth always wants it open, even though Mom always wants it closed. Mom likes privacy, and she doesn't like most people. She's sitting in her chair in the corner, as far away from Ruth as she can get in the little room. She's not reading anything, she's just resting her head in her hands with her eyes closed.

Every spring before Mom goes to the mind hospital, she has to go to the body hospital first so the doctors can fix the wounds she made. They stick some silver tools in her, including knives, but in a helping way, not a destroying way like Mom does to herself. Then, they sew her up like she's a Raggedy Ann doll. I do not like dolls. They creep me out. They watch me all night with their eyes that never close. When Mom's strong enough to walk a little, the doctors send her to the basement for three weeks. She wears bandages around her belly, covering the new scars she keeps adding to the old ones. Her stomach is like a red tattoo, copying one of those museum paintings that don't look like anything and that Grandpa hates.

"Hi, Ruth," I say. Grandma says it too.

"Come give me a hug, Anna," Ruth says. I look at Mom. She still has her eyes closed, like Grandma and I aren't even here. I go hug Ruth, even though I don't like it when adults think they can just get hugs from me whenever they want. Ruth is older than Mom and less crazy. At least, she acts less crazy. Crazy people come in all shapes and sizes, though. Sometimes you can't even tell.

Ruth goes back to reading the magazine. I go over to Mom. "Hi, Mom," I say.

She lifts her head. "Hi, Anna." She takes my hand in hers. "That's funny, I thought you were gone."

I shake my head. "Nope." Here we go again.

Grandma comes over and puts her hand on Mom's shoulder. "Let's not talk about that right now, honey," she says to Mom.

"Oh, shut up, Violet." That's what Mom calls Grandma, even though she's her mom. Grandma says this is disrespectful but Mom does it anyway. Mom turns to me. "I'm so sorry, Anna. I hope I didn't hurt you."

"Not at all," I say. I spin around to show her my body, that nothing is broken. "I'm fine."

"Oh," she says. "Good."

Grandma asks Mom, "How was your day today, Hailey? What did you do?"

Mom shrugs. "Same stuff as yesterday. Group counseling, individual counseling, Bingo, yada yada yada." Mom turns to me again. "Anna, it's not you I want to hurt. I was just confused. Who I really want to hurt, actually kill, is the bad guy."

I try not to roll my eyes. Here we go again. The bad guy is someone Mom talks about only when she is crazy. I don't know who he is. Probably he's not even real. One thing crazy people do is make stuff up that's not real, then think about it so much that they start to believe it. When you're a child, you can believe in things that aren't real and people think it's cute, but when you're an adult, it's not cute, it's just crazy. For example, I have an imaginary boyfriend, Peter, but it's okay because I'm only ten, plus I know he's imaginary.

"Let's not talk about that right now, Hailey," says Grandma. Then she mouths the word "Anna" while pointing at me. She is trying to say that I'm a child, so Mom shouldn't talk about killing people. But I'm used to it. I've seen TV before.

"You never want to talk, Violet," says Mom. "Not about anything that matters."

Grandma frowns. Then she asks Mom, "How are the meds?"

Mom sighs. "Same as always. They make me tired, so tired." She rests her head on her chin. "I feel like I'm in a dream."

"Well, I guess all meds have side effects," Grandma says.

"I guess," says Mom. She looks at me. "I love you, Anna."

"I love you too, Mom." I hug her. She closes her eyes and smiles.

Grandma takes a deck of cards out of her purse and we play Go Fish for the rest of visiting hour. Ruth doesn't want to play. She flips pages of her magazine.

On the outside of our house, the grey paint is peeling. The paint got so old that it turned into pieces of bark flaking off the wooden house. Grandma says Grandpa should paint it, since he paints houses as a job, but he doesn't want to, so it just peels more and more, like dead, dry skin. I used to pick off the pieces to find out what was underneath, but then Grandma saw me and got mad. The house is grey but the door is faded red. The snow's melted now, but the grass in the yard is still dead. There's mud everywhere, and no flowers. Even in summer, nobody waters the lawn, and our grass is always dead.

The inside walls are also grey, except in the bedroom I share with Mom, where they are pink. Mom painted them when she was sixteen, when she found out she was having a baby girl. She has lived in this bedroom her whole life, and I've lived here my whole life too. The pink room is like a heart or a womb that holds us both inside, safe and warm, but also stuck together too close. There are two beds, two dressers, two desks, and two trunks. There is no curtain dividing the halves.

Our house has an upstairs and a downstairs. Upstairs is our room, Grandma and Grandpa's room, and the bathroom. Downstairs is the living room, kitchen, and table where we eat. There's a backyard where Sally the chihuahua plays. Behind the back yard is the woods where I play. I don't know what is behind the woods, because they seem to go on forever. A stream runs through the woods, surrounded by blackberry bushes. I'm not allowed to go past the place where the bushes make a wall across the stream. Mom used to play in the same woods when she was a child.

We have a garage where Grandpa parks his car and Mom cuts herself up every spring. In the garage there is also a bunch of garbage and cardboard boxes with words written in black marker, like "CHRISTMAS" or "VHS." VHS is something that's too old to fit in our TV. The boxes take up room and Grandma has to park her car in the driveway, even in winter when it takes forever to dig it out of the snow. Mom doesn't have a car and neither do I. Grown-ups can get in cars whenever they want and just drive away. Children can't. Neither can Mom. Mom counts as an adult because of her age, but it's like she's not quite an adult, because of her behavior.

When Grandma and I get home from the mind hospital, we eat the dinner Grandpa cooked. Chicken and waffles. Grandpa visited the South once and now this is his favorite meal. I love this food, but at school we learned sugar and fats are bad, and it is necessary to eat vegetables and lean meats instead, like grilled chicken instead of fried chicken. Grandpa does not think so. He's fifty. Whenever I disagree with him, about the vegetables or anything else, he says *I am older than you, Anna,* and to him, this means he is right automatically.

"Pass the syrup, please," Grandpa says to me. Sally sits on the floor next to his chair, wagging her tail and putting her paws on his legs, begging for chicken. Sally is nice but Mom says nobody ever trained her to act right, so she acts crazy. Luckily, she is too small to jump up on the table. I pass Grandpa the bottle of Mrs. Butterworth's, which is shaped like a woman in an apron. He pours the syrup on like crazy, all over the waffles and the chicken. I ask for the bottle back and look at the nutrition facts.

"Do you know how much sugar is in this?" I ask. Grandpa could stand to shed a few pounds. In Phys Ed we play a game where some children are fat cells and other children are regular cells. The game is just tag but with science mixed in. It is meant to teach us to fear fat cells.

Grandpa talks with his mouth full. "I don't know or care," he says. "I'm an old man." He isn't that old. "Sugar is one of the few pleasures in life. I'll eat all the sugar I want."

I shrug. Whatever floats your boat. I imagine Grandpa in a boat, rowing through a river of syrup. I eat my own chicken and waffles plain.

"How was Hailey?" Grandpa asks Grandma.

"She seemed fine," says Grandma. "Tired."

Grandpa sighs. "She's always tired. What does she have to be tired about? She's only twenty-four. I'm fifty and I have more energy than her."

"The meds make her tired, Hank," says Grandma.

"Maybe she should stop taking the meds, then." He stuffs his mouth up with more waffle. "She could help around the house when she comes home. Get a job again."

"She can't stop taking the meds. You know that."

"Well, they don't seem to help, do they? This keeps happening."

"Hank," Grandma says, then points to me and mouths my name again. "Maybe we can talk about this later."

"Oh, all right," he says. "How is school, Anna?"

"Fine," I say.

"What did you learn today?"

I shrug. "Nothing."

"Nothing? Why are we sending you to school, then?"

"It's the law," I say. "You have to go to school until you're sixteen."

"Nonsense," he says. "I dropped out when I was only fourteen. I helped my parents with the farm. I did *real* work." The rules were probably different back then, or maybe he was breaking the rules and nobody noticed. I decide not to bother saying this.

"School *is* real work," says Grandma. "Anna got her mid-term report card. Straight fours." She pats me on the back. "I'm so proud of her."

"What is a *four?*" asks Grandpa.

"It's like an A," I say.

"Well, why don't they just call it an A?"

"I don't know. I didn't make the rules." I take my last bite of waffle and wipe my mouth with the napkin like Grandma tells me to do. "Thank you for dinner, Grandpa."

I start clearing off the table so I can do the dishes. "There you go, real work," he says. "That's what I like to see."

Sally lays on my bed with me while I write in my notebook. I've done this every night since I was six, when Mom gave me my first notebook. She writes in notebooks too. Some people call them *diaries*, but boys at school make fun of that word so now I just say *notebook*.

There's a knock on the bedroom door. "May I come in?" asks Grandma, and then she comes in before I can answer. "It's time to turn the light out and go to sleep, Anna," she says.

From down the hall Grandpa's voice says, "I can't afford to be paying out my ass for electricity!" Ass is a curse word. I learned so at school. Grandpa says cursing is also one of the few pleasures in life. Curse words are words that adults are allowed to say, but not children.

Grandma comes over and kisses me on the forehead. Sally barks. Grandma leaves the door open a little so Sally can leave my room when she wants. Sally is like a baby, she doesn't sleep through the night.

Every night I say a prayer, even though I secretly think God's not real. I've thought about it, and it just doesn't make sense. If God made the world, who made God? Why do bad things happen? How does he live on top of clouds, which are made of gas and not solid? Still, I pray just in case, and because it's a habit.

Mom says I have to close my eyes when I pray because it shows God that you're focused on the prayer, not distracted. But sometimes even though I close my eyes, I think of other things and forget I'm praying. When this happens, I say sorry to God. And sometimes I fall asleep before I say *Amen*.

In my prayers, I list people who I want God to protect. I'm scared that if I forget anybody, something bad will happen to them. It takes me a long time. Then even after I spend a long time, I'm scared I forgot someone, so I ask Him to keep everyone in the whole world safe.

I also pray for Peter. I can't remember how long he's been around. He's eleven. I like older men, like the woman on *The Bachelorette*, Grandma's favorite TV show. *I'm sick of boys. So immature,* the woman said. *I need a real man.* Peter's not real though. He plays with me during the day, but only when Grandma and Grandpa aren't around. Sometimes he's in my dreams. Sometimes not.

The next day after school, I ask Grandma if I can go outside. "Sure," she says, not looking up from the TV. She is watching *The*

Bachelorette. On this show, they are all real people, not pretend like most of TV.

I go outside and walk into the woods.

The woods are a maze of trees. There are trails of dirt. If you go off the trails, you're in the real wild.

The trees are tall and covered in new leaves for spring. Except the pine trees, those are always green. Moss covers some of the trees, and birds fly between them like they're searching for the perfect tree to build their homes in. Squirrels too. If I go back far enough in the woods I find the stream. That's where I always meet Peter, my imaginary boyfriend. Sometimes, we play witches. Other times we get into the stream and walk, see what we can find. Tadpoles live in the stream, which grow up into frogs. The only fish are tiny and silver like needles. I've never gone past the place I'm not supposed to go past, where the blackberry bushes make a wall across the stream. Mom says that's where the bad guy lives. Grandma says the bad guy's not real but it's dangerous back there just the same.

I hear things in the woods that I can't identify. There are howls, breathing, screams, purring, growling, songs, whispers. Animals or monsters. Monsters are just animals that humans haven't discovered yet.

Peter shows up to the stream wearing a T-shirt. On the shirt, he has drawn a big tree, but all the leaves are hearts. Peter's parents buy him blank T-shirts and special markers you can use to draw on clothes so the picture doesn't come off when you wash it. Peter is an artist. He is skinny like how I want to be. Grandma says men get metabolism they don't deserve, same with long eyelashes. Peter's eyelashes are as long as the legs of house centipedes, but not scary. His hair is blue, because his parents let him dye it. They let him do whatever he wants. That's because they're imaginary.

Peter helps me collect eight sticks, one for each new emotion. Tomorrow I will take the sticks to school and color each one the right color with markers during free time. We don't have any markers at home.

Peter kisses my cheek and I blush. At least I think I do, that's what they say happens on TV. I ask him if I blush.

"Of course you do," he says. He kisses my cheek again, where I'm blushing.

I wonder if I should wear blush like adults. That's a kind of makeup. "Do you think I'm pretty?" I ask Peter.

"You're the prettiest girl in the world," he says.

Peter's nice. "You're the handsomest boy in the world," I say. I kiss him on the cheek, too.

We decide to make a potion. We dig a hole in the ground to use as a mixing bowl. We gather all the different materials we can find: mud, leaves, pine needles, an unripe berry, small shavings of bark, and a worm. We have made all kinds of potions before: a love potion (which was kind of pointless, because we are already in love), a poison (which we never used), and a potion to make us happy (that one worked).

Today we create a potion that will make any wish come true. I stir the ingredients with a large stick, except the worm.

"I'll put the worm in," Peter says.

"No, don't do it," I say. "The worm will suffocate or drown."

"But we need him for the potion."

"No, we don't."

"Do you want the potion to work?"

"Yes."

"Then we need him."

Killing is wrong, I think, not out loud but in my head.

"Killing is usually wrong," Peter says, "but it's more complicated than that." Peter can read my thoughts, because he's imaginary, which means he lives inside my head. I don't know why I even bother speaking out loud. I worry I'm getting a little old for imaginary friends or boyfriends. Soon I will be a teenager, then an adult, then a senior citizen, almost dead.

Peter says, "For example, we kill animals to eat them."

"I don't kill the animals," I say.

"Someone does."

"I guess you're right, someone does."

"And a worm is an animal. Killing an animal is less of a big deal than killing a human."

"Why?"

"It just is."

I shrug. "Mom wants to kill the bad man," I say.

"Yes," he says. "Killing is complicated. If he's bad, maybe it's okay to kill him even if he is a human. Like how they killed Osama Bin Laden."

"I guess."

"So," Peter says, "I'll put the tadpole in." He drops the tadpole into the hole in the ground. I don't stop him. I mix the potion. I stab the tadpole with my stick. It's the biggest thing I've ever killed, so far.

When the potion is ready, Peter drinks some. "I wish to live forever," he says.

"I wish—" I say, but I'm too embarrassed to say it out loud, even though Peter can hear me either way. In my head I say, *I wish Mom never tries to cut me out of her belly again.*

Peter smiles. I drink the potion and nearly throw up.

We say goodbye. Peter walks across the stream to the other side, the place I'm not allowed to go. That's where Peter lives too, there and inside my brain. I watch him walk until he's a tiny dot in the distance, and he disappears behind some trees. I think I see a flash of another face, with long hair like moss. It's a woman's face, sort of like Mom's. It scares me and I look away. When I look back, she is gone.

Before I go to sleep, I look out my window and see two full moons in the sky. I blink and look again, but there's still two. They're identical. They shine equally bright, like two big cat's eyes. I don't know which is the regular one and which is new. I point them out to Sally and she barks.

"Grandma!" I call, and Grandma runs in.

"Is everything okay?" she asks.

"There are two moons in the sky," I say, pointing.

Grandma looks out the window. "Don't be silly," she says. "That's just one moon, like always."

I frown. "Sally saw it," I say.

"Sally's a dumb dog," Grandma says.

"You can say that again!" yells Grandpa from across the hall. "Go to bed, Anna."

Grandma kisses my forehead and leaves.

I look at Mom's empty bed. There's no curtain so I divide our room in half with an invisible witch force. We keep our own things on our own sides: books, toys, clothes. Even when Mom's gone, I keep my things on my side. I suddenly realize this is stupid. I take my Raggedy Ann doll and carry it to Mom's bed. I tuck her in with her face turned down on the pillow, so she can't watch me. I pray, and ask God to explain the two moons to me, and also everything else.

It's Easter Sunday, so the mind hospital has longer visiting hours and a special event. They do this every Easter. It's kind of like at school on holidays, where it's a regular day except we also eat cupcakes and do an art project. But some kid or other always finds something to cry about, and ruins the fun. Sometimes I wonder why people bother with special events at all.

Pink and yellow streamers hang on the walls of the big lunch room, which is also the group therapy room and the special event room. On the long grey tables there are plastic bins full of old colored pencils and crayons mixed together, and coloring sheets: Easter eggs and rabbits. A song about Jesus plays out of an old boombox in the corner. Already, one patient is yelling next to the boombox. "I am not a Christian!" he says. "This music is offensive to me!" A nurse goes to the boombox and changes the CD

to a Halloween mix. "The Monster Mash" comes on. The patient
smiles and goes back to coloring his rabbit.

"Do you want to color a picture, Anna?" asks Grandma.

"Sure," I say. I'm okay at coloring, but not great. Mom is
great, but she never does it anymore, so it doesn't matter that she's
great. I choose the rabbit because it will take longer. I'm glad to
have something to do.

"Do you think Jesus really rose from the dead?" Mom asks.

"Of course not," says Grandpa, who came with us today
because it's Easter. "What are you, five? Everyone knows that
story's a load of crap."

"Hank!" Grandma says, and hits him on the arm. "Yes, sweetie,
Jesus really rose from the dead."

"I'm not saying he wasn't a nice guy and all," Grandpa says,
"just that they embellished the story a little. You know, to help
with book sales."

Grandma hits him again. I laugh a little, then cover my mouth
when I see Grandma glaring at me. A patient at the other end of
our long table gets a paper cut, and a nurse rushes over to clean up
the blood and make sure he didn't do it on purpose.

"What do you think, Anna?" Mom asks.

I look at my coloring sheet to avoid making eye contact with
anyone. "Well," I say, "It doesn't seem real that someone could
rise from the dead, but I'm not a doctor."

Mom laughs a little.

"Maybe some people are magic," I say. "Like witches."

"Jesus was the son of Mary," says Grandma.

"Oh yeah? And who was the father?" asks Grandpa.

"God."

"I mean the *human* father."

"He didn't have one."

"How can *that* be?"

The man who got a papercut butts in. "I don't have a human
father."

Grandpa frowns. "Everyone has a human mother and a human father. It's science! Even if you never met them, you still—"

"Hank!" Grandma hits him again. She turns to the man. "I'm sorry. My husband never learned to control his manners."

The man shrugs. "It's okay."

I am really glad to have my picture. I'm coloring it as slowly as I can. Grandma keeps glancing at me like she is nervous I'll get sad about never meeting my "father." I don't care about any father. I don't have one.

Some hospital kitchen workers come through the doors with two silver carts full of cupcakes. Several patients cry out in a happy way. It's just like school. A few people get up and go straight for the carts.

"Calm down," says one of the nurses, holding out her hand like a stop sign. "We'll form a line here. There's no need to panic. Everyone will get a cupcake."

The nurses hand each person a paper plate and a napkin with hearts on it, leftover from Valentine's Day. I wait until everyone else has gone before I take Mom's hand and we go get our cupcakes.

"Well, aren't you polite," says the nurse, smiling at me.

I shrug.

"She's so sweet," the nurse says to Mom. Mom pats me on the back.

Peter and I leave our shoes under a tree and wade through the creek. We do this often. The further along we go, away from all the houses, the deeper the creek gets, the more wild the surroundings. Stranger and louder noises from animals, thicker trees, colder. There are more and more blackberry bushes growing along the sides of the stream, covered in thorns. They grow in towards the stream and above our heads, crowd us in like a tunnel. We continue until the blackberry bushes from the left and the right come together in a wall in front of us, keeping us out of whatever lies beyond. The only way to get past the wall would be to swim underneath, and even if we did that we'd still get scratched.

On our walks through the creek we always find interesting items: ripped pages with the words smudged out, beer cans and cigarette buts, a tire, and once even a doll's head.

"Peter," I say, "did you see the two moons in the sky last night?"

"Yes," he said. "Of course. How could I miss them?"

"Nobody else saw them," I said.

"Hmm."

"Maybe they're imaginary."

"Or," he said, "maybe they're real, but only we can see them."

"Maybe," I say, to be polite, even though that is ridiculous. "Why do you think there are two?"

"Maybe the regular moon found a friend. Or she had a baby."

I shrug. We are almost to the end. "Peter," I say, "Should I swim under today?"

"Your Grandma will get mad," he says. "You'll get your sweater wet, not just your pants."

"I don't care," I say.

He says nothing.

"What's back there?" I ask. But, of course, he doesn't know. Even if he does live there, he's not even real. He only knows what I know.

The blackberry bushes become transparent, and I think I see a woman's face peeking out from behind a distant tree again, her hair like moss. She looks like Mom. She sees me and pulls her face back all the way behind the tree. But her arm sticks out and points right at me, then points towards the place where the blackberry bushes meet.

I take a deep breath and dive in.

Underwater, it's like I'm in a cave, floating in the liquid, but I can't breathe. I have to hold my breath, otherwise choke until I die.

Shiny little fish swim around me, like knives bending in the light. They turn into knives with faces. They all look at me like I'm meat to be cut up, my heart roasted over a fire. They look at me and lick their lips. Here they come.

PHEROMONES

MARGOT HONESTLY DIDN'T HATE her job. Not the way other adults seemed to hate theirs, with passion and purpose and some sense of what they'd do instead if the opportunity were only given to them. Margot felt sorry for the girls she worked with, but not so sorry that she was willing to quit. Margot worked for a company that offered modeling classes to preteens. It was not a modeling agency, and was not affiliated with one, and in no way guaranteed the girls would ever get modeling work. Anyone at all could sign up for the classes, no matter what she looked like. Margot taught the girls how to walk on the runway, how to fix their hair and apply makeup (which, if they ever became models, they would not be doing themselves anyway), how to pose for photographs in the most flattering ways. Margot knew none of these girls would ever get modeling jobs, and that the whole thing was a scam. She hated seeing those preteens' hopeful faces on the first day of class, their braces and acne shining under bright lights.

Like most of the others who worked at the company, Margot had once been a model. Not one of the rich and famous runway models, but she was in department store catalogues and a few TV commercials for hand lotion. Occasionally Margot would still get gigs, but not as often now. Working for this company provided her with a steadier paycheck, anyway, which was important now that she was a mother. Margot was thankful that her own daughter, Sam, who was twelve, had never shown any interest in modeling. Sam was interested in science and soccer and having her hair cut short. Margot wished she had been like Sam when she was younger. She admired her daughter very much.

Margot had now decided it was a waste of time for women to put any thought into their appearances. She still put thought into her own appearance; she couldn't help it after all these years. But she wanted to deter others from making the same mistake. She wanted to grab each mother who signed her daughter up for these classes by the shoulders, shake them, and say, "Listen. I know what I'm talking about. Sign your kid up for the Science Olympiad instead. We need more women in STEM." And she wanted the mothers to smile and listen to her and turn their daughters away. They'd save their money and buy a chemistry set or a puppy instead. They'd stop looking at their daughters as just profit-makers.

Kelly, Margot's wife, was a scientist too. A marine biologist. Kelly never wore makeup or straightened her hair or worried about what angle her face was at in photographs, yet she still happened to be very beautiful. She always got a lot of attention, from men and women alike. Margot had always been jealous of this. Kelly didn't seem to care what she looked like or how much attention she got. Margot got attention too, but she worked for it. She had spent her whole life working to look good, and still she only looked as good as Kelly, not better. Kelly had her beauty *and* her career. Margot's were one and the same.

Margot was Sam's birth mom. Kelly had explained that she was a little butch for pregnancy. Margot's body had changed after pregnancy, and she didn't like that. Her breasts drooped a little more, her waist was a little larger. And she was aging. Margot had always thought somehow that her body would stay the same until she was sixty. Maybe it was the way women looked on television.

But she was only forty-five and already her hair was thinning and her back was hunching over like she was half-dead. At least it felt that way to her. Kelly assured her she was just as beautiful as ever, and that she loved her very much.

Margot was teaching the girls how to pick the right foundation color. "Take the bottle and hold it to your wrist," she said. "If it looks close, use your Q-tip to put a streak of the liquid on your wrist. See if it matches."

The girls obeyed. She had ten students in the class today. They passed around the bottles and smiled as they found matches.

"Now I'm going to show you how to put it on," Margot said. No preteen should have to worry about foundation, she thought. She passed out sponges and brushes and made sure each girl had her own chair and her own mirror. She walked around and made sure everyone was doing it right, blending it at the jawline to prevent a line between face and neck, dusting setting powder over their faces when they were done.

Several of the girls had terrible acne. They were preteens. Still, Margot thought, they shouldn't have to worry about foundation. Boys didn't have to. Foundation was a waste of time and money, plus it clogged your pores and made your skin even worse. Nobody's acne would heal if they caked foundation over it every day. These girls could be reading books or kicking soccer balls instead of doing this bullshit. In a vain attempt to help them, Margot said to the class, "I know this is fun, but always remember that school is first, modeling second."

Margot and Kelly went to a party for Kelly's co-worker Anne's birthday. They were good friends with Anne. She also happened to also be very beautiful, and gay, and single. She had recently divorced her wife Donna because Donna had been cheating on her. This, even though Anne was so beautiful. There is no justice in the world, Margot thought.

Anne was turning forty. There was a cake that said "Over the Hill" with a frosted picture of a tombstone on it. Anne laughed, but Margot shuddered. She would have killed someone if they'd given her an "Over the Hill" cake for her own fortieth birthday.

It seemed all of Kelly's co-workers were present. Anne was very popular, even more so since her divorce. People believed she needed support. Sam played with Anne's daughter, Abigail. Abigail was five, and Sam loved playing dolls with her even though she'd never liked dolls herself, but Abigail was cute. "I want to be a mom," Sam said to Margot. Margot slapped herself on the forehead.

Anne didn't want to cut the cake, so Kelly did it for her. Anne laughed and put her hand on Kelly's shoulder. Kelly smiled at her.

Margot was teaching the girls how to pose for photographs. "Make sure to smile," she said. "Tilt your head so that you catch the light. Use the light for contouring; it's more effective than makeup. Don't scrunch your forehead." The girls did everything she said. "Stand up straight with your shoulders back, and bend one leg slightly out. It's slimming." No preteen should have to worry about slimming herself in photographs, Margot thought. They should just worry about becoming good people. Margot imagined these same girls at a birthday party, catching the light with their bad skin and sticking one leg too far out.

After class, the mothers came to pick their daughters up. One student's mother stayed to speak to Margot. "I wanted to ask you about plus size modeling," she said. Her daughter, Michelle, was overweight, even obese according to the BMI scale. Michelle stood a few feet away from the women, as if giving them privacy, but she was still within hearing distance. Margot nodded. The mother asked questions, but Margot didn't want to answer any of them, and she especially did not want to tell this mother that most plus-size models did not even wear plus sizes, but instead wore between size 6-12, which is still smaller than the average size for an American woman, which is 14-16.

And so instead Margot said, "these are all wonderful questions. Let me get you a pamphlet about our special plus-size modeling class from my office. Michelle could enroll next season, once our current class is over."

The mother smiled and nodded. "Oh, that would be lovely. Thank you so much, Margot. This class really means the world to Michelle." She paused for a moment, then whispered very quietly, "you know, she's had terrible confidence issues in the past."

Margot smiled and nodded back. She walked towards her office, passing Michelle on the way. The girl was beaming, like Christmas morning.

"I want to be a mother," Sam said at the dinner table. She scooped herself an extra helping of mashed potatoes. Margot was glad she wasn't worried about her weight.

"That's nice," said Kelly.

"But don't forget about being a scientist," said Margot.

"Oh, I won't," said Sam. "Mom's a mother and a scientist." Kelly smiled. Margot didn't know why she'd assumed Sam was giving up her dream of becoming a scientist to pursue the dream of becoming a mother.

After dinner, Kelly took a phone call and stepped outside to talk. She didn't normally do this. Margot washed the dishes while Sam did homework. Margot watched Kelly out the window, touching her face and laughing. Kelly looked like a schoolgirl with a crush.

When Kelly came inside, Margot said, "Who was it?"

Kelly wiped the smile off her face. She shrugged. "Just Anne," she said. "She had a question about work."

"You sure were laughing a lot for a work question," she said.

Kelly frowned at her. "I don't know what you're talking about."

"You sure were laughing a lot at her party, too."

"It's nothing," Kelly said, and gave Margot a kiss.

Before the girls arrived at modeling class, Margot's boss came in to talk to her. "Why did you tell Mrs. Wright that you didn't know anything about plus size modeling?" she asked.

Margot sighed. "I'm sorry," she said. "I didn't want to depress her."

"You should have told her it's great!" she said. "Do you think she's going to sign Michelle up for the advanced class if you discourage her?"

"I wasn't trying to discourage her," Margot said. "Just being realistic."

"Well, you weren't realistic. You were just unhelpful." Her boss held eye contact for a few seconds without saying anything. "Don't let it happen again."

"Yes, of course," said Margot. Her boss walked out of the room.

Sam was preparing a project for the Science Olympiad, about pheromones. Sam was fascinated by the idea that what attracted two people to each other was not some elusive sort of magic, but a chemical that could be scientifically explained. Sam liked logic and rationality and math. Margot had never liked the idea of pheromones, and preferred not to believe in them. She liked the idea that love was magic. She found the idea of pheromones reductive and depressing.

Margot drove Sam to the craft store to buy supplies for the project. "I need a big poster board," said Sam. "The kind with three panels." Sam also apparently needed a special kind of marker, even though they already owned markers that Margot thought were just fine.

At home, Sam drew a man on the left panel and a woman on the right panel. In the center panel, she drew the pheromones, even though they are invisible. She drew them as tiny clouds with hearts for eyes and arms reaching out towards each other. She printed out her descriptions of how pheromones work and pasted the descriptions next to the drawings. She wrote the word "PHEROMONES" very large at the top.

"I'm so proud of you," Kelly said, and kissed Sam's head. "My little scientist."

"How come it's a man and a woman?" Margot asked. "Why not two women or two men?"

Kelly glared at her. Sam shrugged.

In the bedroom, Kelly asked Margot, "Why did you say that? Why did you ask Sam about the man and the woman?"

"I don't want her to be so heteronormative," Margot said. "She has two moms, and she still drew a straight couple. I don't want her to be like everyone else."

"She's not like everyone else," Kelly said. "She's special."

Margot frowned.

Kelly took her hand. "Sorry," she said. "I understand what you mean. I just don't think it was that big of a deal. Some couples are straight, after all."

"Yeah," said Margot. And some couples are gay. "Do you think Sam is straight?"

"I don't know. But I love her either way."

Margot drove Sam to the Science Olympiad. Her schedule was more open than Kelly's, since her job was only part-time. Sam sat in the backseat with her giant poster, reading the words over and over and smiling. Right now, Kelly was at work, with Anne, Margot thought. She didn't want to think about pheromones, science, or Kelly.

They arrived at school and set up Sam's poster at a table in the cafeteria. Other kids set up their own projects about dinosaurs, volcanoes, and deep-sea exploration. Sam's was certainly the most unique, Margot thought. The least obvious choice for a twelve-year old. A few teachers walked around looking at the projects and nodding their heads.

Margot went to use the restroom. While she urinated, she took her pocket mirror out of her purse and checked her makeup. She had always done this: checked and reapplied makeup in bathroom stalls. She was too embarrassed to do it in the mirror above the sink, since others could see her. She didn't know why this was. She supposed she didn't want anyone to know it took her so much effort to look pretty. She wanted everyone to think she was like Kelly, effortlessly and naturally beautiful. Margot felt like a fraud, but she'd rather be a fraud than ugly. She smoothed some powder onto the sponge and dabbed the shiny parts of her face.

When Margot returned from the restroom, Kelly was there. "I didn't know you were coming," said Margot.

Kelly smiled. "I got off early," she said.

The teachers walked around judging projects. They asked the children questions, then wrote things down on their clipboards. Margot didn't like the idea of this judging. She didn't like the idea of winners and losers and rankings, not anymore. She had liked that idea when she was younger, when she could have won a beauty contest. She didn't want Sam to lose.

But Sam did lose. She got third place, after the dinosaurs and the volcanoes. "The volcanoes?" Margot said. "Seriously?" The volcano project included a baking soda and vinegar volcano. It wasn't even dyed red. "Everyone does that experiment in like second grade."

"Shh," Kelly said, and nudged Margot with her elbow.

Sam looked at the ground and shrugged. "Oh, well," she said. Then she went over to congratulate the winner.

"Are you having an affair with Anne?" Margot asked Kelly.

"What are you talking about?"

"Just that. Are you having an affair?"

"What?" Kelly said. "No. I would never. You know that."

Margot was silent.

"Don't you know that?" Kelly asked.

Margot looked at the floor.

"Margot," Kelly said, "I love you. I would never have an affair, not with Anne, not with anyone. I promise." Kelly touched Margot's chin and tipped it up so that they looked into each other's eyes. Margot blinked.

It was graduation day at the modeling class. The girls were to perform a series of tasks in front of an audience of parents, then each girl would be presented with a certificate of participation. Some people said this generation was being ruined by participation trophies. Margot generally disagreed, but in this case she agreed.

After the makeup and the hair and the posing for photographs, the girls filed out from behind a curtain onto the catwalk, wearing outfits that expressed their favorite fashion trends: leather jackets, tea dresses, cowgirl boots. They each paused at the front and turned from side to side with their heads raised. The parents cheered and snapped photos. Margot could tell some of them still harbored hopes about their daughters becoming real models. They snapped the photos and pretended to be professional photographers hired to cover a big London or New York City fashion show. But this was a suburb of Seattle, and none of these girls would ever be famous, or even rich, or even happy, probably. Margot sighed.

The girls lined up and grasped hands while Margot said some

words to the parents. "Thank you for enrolling your daughters in our class," she said. "We believe everyone is beautiful and everyone is special." The girls all smiled. The lights shone bright on their faces, and they looked like children who had been playing with their mothers' makeup, which is exactly what they were, only somewhere along the line, the play had turned into a hellish reality.

Margot handed each girl their certificate of participation. Each girl shook hands with Margot and then went to sit down with her parents. After one more round of applause, everyone started to file out.

"You did well," said Margot's boss. She put her hand on Margot's shoulder.

"Thanks," Margot said. She may have done well, but she'd done well at a bad thing. "I don't think I want to do this anymore," she said.

"Why?"

"It's just not right for me," Margot said. "It's just not right."

Her boss frowned, then opened her mouth to speak, but Margot just turned and left the place.

In the car, Margot watched the shadows of red traffic lights bloom on the wet pavement. She waited. She counted the seconds that went by as she sat at the red light, and she took note that these were wasted seconds. Life was too short, it went by too quickly. She looked over into the car next to her and lowered her window, to try to communicate this to the other driver. But the other driver didn't see her. "Don't you see what's wrong with this picture?" Margot asked. She waved her arms, then continued to talk in the direction of the woman in the next car. "We're sitting at this red light, and nobody's even coming the other way. We're wasting our lives. Time is precious." But Margot didn't even believe the words coming out of her mouth, not really. Was time really precious? She didn't know. She only knew that there was something very wrong with the world, and she didn't know how to fix it, and she didn't know who to ask for help. Girls were dying of anorexia and the advertisements full of exclusively thin women kept coming. That was enough to prove people were heartless. Plus, bombs were going off and people were starving, or whatever. Margot didn't really follow the news about foreign countries. She saw enough problems in her immediate surroundings. "Something's wrong with the world," Margot said to the other driver.

The other driver suddenly noticed Margot talking in her direction. She lowered her own window and asked, "What did you say?"

Margot paused. "Nothing," she said. The light turned green and both women drove on.

MY LIFE IS THE SIZE OF A WALNUT

CAROLINE AND JOHN NEVER told each other much about their pasts, their families, or the reasons why they were the way they were. They had an unspoken agreement that their relationship was a new phase for both of them, and they preferred to leave the past behind. They knew and loved each other now, and that was all that mattered.

John was Caroline's supervisor at the office, and everyone thought he was handsome and charismatic. Caroline was shy and sad all the time, and she thought she wasn't pretty but she wasn't ugly either. She'd had boyfriends before, but none of them were that great and none of them ever told her they loved her. John and Caroline started seeing each other in secret, because it was against office rules for supervisors to date subordinates. John was kind and he told her she was beautiful and that he loved her, and she decided she'd do anything for him.

When they got engaged they told their coworkers, and despite the rule, everyone thought it was okay because they were engaged and that was more important than anything. They received many cards and presents. After the wedding, they honeymooned on a tropical island, got a dog, and put a down payment on a house. Caroline didn't really like islands or dogs or even houses, but she knew everyone was supposed to like these things, so she pretended.

They smiled at each other and held hands all the time and John bought Caroline flowers when he got a little extra money.

After their daughter Isabelle was born, Caroline stopped going to work. The cost of childcare made her working pointless. Caroline never thought she'd get married or have children, but John wanted a baby so badly that she agreed. Every time the baby drank Caroline's milk, she'd spit or vomit it out, sometimes all the way across the room like she was possessed. John laughed even though it wasn't funny. The doctor said the only reason babies would reject breast milk was if the mother was eating something the baby was allergic to. But he ran tests, and Isabelle wasn't allergic to anything at all. John bought baby formula and fed the baby himself.

Caroline could tell John loved their daughter more than anything, including Caroline. But Caroline loved John more than the baby. She didn't tell this to anyone. She had some friends, but she wasn't close enough with any of them to discuss that sort of thing. She wasn't close with her family, either. Caroline thought that because John loved the baby so much, it would be better if he stayed home and she went to work, but she couldn't make as much money as him, even though she had a college degree and he didn't. She had thought a college degree was a financial investment. But at least in her case, not much good ever came out of getting one.

On the weekends, John would wander through the rooms and dust the surface of each piece of furniture and scrub the sinks and the insides of kitchen appliances, even though Caroline always did the cleaning during the week when Isabelle was sleeping. Apparently, her cleaning was not good enough for him. "Sorry," she said. "I'm not exactly Suzie Homemaker."

John kissed her and said, "It's okay, sweetheart. I love you."

After he cleaned, he'd go into the garage and the yard and find things that he thought needed fixing, then fix them. He'd insist on cooking meals, even though Caroline could cook fine. She thought he didn't like her cooking. She didn't really like his cooking, either. He used too much pepper and too many spices. She never told him this.

After a few months, Caroline and John decided to go to their coworker's Christmas party at a bar, and leave the baby for the first time. They did not have money to throw away on childcare and John's parents lived closer than Caroline's (hers were in another state). They took the baby to John's parents' house for the night.

Caroline did not know John's parents very well. His mother dyed her hair red and wore cheetah print blouses and too much eyeliner that bled underneath her eyes like black watercolor, and she always had a lot of Boston terriers. Recently she had begun trying to breed them. When John and Caroline walked into the house she said, "Let me show you something." She led them into the kitchen where, on the counter, she had laid out a litter of dead newborn puppies as if they were something she'd baked that needed to cool off. "Aren't they beautiful?" she asked. Their eyes were just little closed slits, never opened, and their velvet hair shined like a sad, open eye. To Caroline, they looked peaceful. She reached out her hand to touch one, then realized what she was doing and shot her hand back to her chest.

John's father sat in a chair in the living room, and didn't say anything about the dead puppies. He was always quieter than his wife. He'd been in the military and kept his appearance neat. Although he wasn't overly friendly, he seemed like a reasonable person, not like his wife, who Caroline thought was a bit stupid and a bit crazy too.

"Hi, John!" said John's brother Kyle, coming out of his bedroom. Kyle wore sweatpants all the time and played too many video games and lived with his parents even though he was an adult. He had some sort of addiction and seemed to have suffered brain damage, but Caroline didn't know the details. "Is that the baby?" he said, even though the thing Catherine held was obviously a baby and he had also met her before. Kyle lunged too quickly and clumsily towards the bundle in Caroline's arms. The baby began to cry, and Kyle recoiled.

As the couple left, John's father stood up and said quietly to Caroline, "Don't worry. We'll take care of her." His voice was deep like the sound a sturdy ship makes, Caroline thought. She passed Isabelle off into his arms.

At the Christmas party Caroline got drunk for the first time in a year. People danced with each other, but Caroline preferred to dance alone. When she squinted her eyes and spun around, the red and green lights in the darkness were like a neon impressionist garden and she was a character in a children's book. Caroline had never felt like an adult, not even now that she was a mother. She enjoyed being drunk because she could act like a child and have an excuse for it. She often watched children in public and envied them, because only children were allowed to have fun openly, only children were allowed to suffer openly.

Caroline got dizzy. She had once read in a book that spinning very fast produced an effect in the brain similar to an intoxicant, and that was why children did it so much. She went to sit down and watch other people dance. Because Caroline wouldn't dance with John, he was dancing with another woman, the woman who'd taken over Caroline's job when Isabelle was born. The woman did not have a husband or boyfriend to bring to the party. Her name was Kelly, and she wasn't particularly ugly or pretty but was just a regular-looking woman, like Caroline. The difference was Kelly applied nail polish and curled her hair every day, unlike Caroline, who just let it dry naturally. She had long ago learned that men either didn't notice or didn't care about things like nail polish or eyeshadow. Other women noticed, though. The other difference between Caroline and Kelly was that Kelly smiled and laughed more than Caroline did and didn't seem to hate herself. Men did notice that.

Caroline got up to use the restroom. In the stall, she saw a piece of graffiti that said: "I am a teenager. My life is the size of a walnut. I don't care about Afghanistan."

"Same," Caroline scribbled underneath with a black pen. She always kept pens in her purse in case she ever came up with a good idea and needed to write it down. She hardly ever needed the pens. This was the first graffiti she'd ever done.

The next morning, Caroline had a headache and felt like she hadn't slept at all, even though she knew she slept more than she usually did because the baby wasn't there. Next time we leave the baby with John's parents, she thought, I'm not going to drink.

"When did I get so old?" she asked John. He laughed from the driver's seat. He always drove when both of them were in the car together. "I used to drink like that every Saturday in college, then go to the library on Sunday and write essays about Shakespeare or James Joyce, with no headache or anything. How did I do that?"

"Beats me," said John. He put his hand on her thigh and smiled.

The dead puppies were no longer on the kitchen counter when they arrived at John's parents' house. How did one dispose of dead puppies? Bury them or just throw them in the trash? Caroline imagined a black garbage bag filled with that soft hair and those slit-eyes.

John spoke with his parents about the Christmas party and how Isabelle did last night, and Kyle pulled Caroline aside. "I wouldn't leave that baby here again if I were you," he said. "Our mother tried to kill me when I was six. She put Drano in my Kool-Aid."

There's no way that's true, Caroline thought. "Why would she want to do that?" she asked.

"Probably she wanted money from the government," he said. "The government gives people money when tragedies like that happen."

"Hmm," she said, and nodded her head to be polite.

He moved past her to put a candy wrapper in the trash can. She thought she saw a tiny dog nose, peeking out from underneath a clean paper towel that had probably been used in attempt to cover it.

Isabelle grew older. She said she didn't like her birth name, the name Caroline had chosen for her, and she asked to be called Cinderella instead. John called her this, but Caroline refused. She did not like the moral of the story "Cinderella."

She was three, then four, then five. She asked to be called Ariel, then Pocahontas, then Mulan. "I want to be a soldier," she said to Caroline. She asked for a toy sword. Caroline wouldn't let John buy her one. Isabelle found a stick in the yard and used it to fight John, who had his own stick.

"Why do you want to be a soldier?" Caroline asked Isabelle.

"I want to be strong," she said. "I want to destroy my enemies."

Isabelle didn't get to see Caroline's parents very often. "Other kids have two grandmas and two grandpas," she said. "How come I only have one of each?"

"You *have* two of each," said Caroline, "you just don't see the others very often."

"Why?"

"Because they live in another state."

"Can we go see them?"

"Maybe someday."

"Can they babysit me instead?"

"Why? What's wrong with the grandparents who babysit you now?"

She didn't answer. "Call me Peter Pan from now on," she said. "I'm going to cut off people's hands and feed them to the alligators." She ran off to sword-fight more with John.

"I want to go to Neverland," Isabelle said at dinner.

"Neverland is a wonderful place, honey," said John.

"Call me *Peter Pan*, Dad, not *honey*."

"Oh, my mistake," he said. "Neverland is wonderful, Peter Pan."

She smiled.

"Why do you want to go to Neverland?" Caroline asked.

"That's where the Lost Boys live. They also have mermaids and pirates."

"But the pirates are bad," Caroline said.

"I know," Isabelle said. She pouted, then smiled. "But I'll cut off their hands and feed them to the alligators!"

"That's not very nice," said John.

"They deserve it," Isabelle hissed. She never hissed.

John frowned.

"They try to kill the Lost Boys. They deserve it. I'll cut off their hands so they can't hold a sword anymore. Let's see them try to kill the Lost Boys then!"

"Why is she so obsessed with killing?" Caroline asked John as they climbed into bed.

"Oh, Caroline, it's just a phase," he said. "All children are obsessed with killing."

"I wasn't," she said.

"Well, you weren't normal," he said. He smiled. She tried to smile. He was trying to flirt with her, he was still trying. He kissed her and they slept together, although Caroline's mind was elsewhere.

"I really wouldn't leave Peter Pan here anymore," Kyle said to Caroline. "My mother tried to kill me when I was seven. She put knives in my pillowcase instead of a pillow. She wanted to stab my brain out of my head."

Caroline shook her head. "No way," she said. She looked over at John's father. He was sitting on the ground with Isabelle, playing with miniature trains. John's mother was in the kitchen mixing Crystal Light, sugar-free Kool-Aid. Isabelle wouldn't drink anything without sugar. She asked for apple juice next to her bed at night instead of water. John encouraged the bad habit. She cried when Caroline tried to give her water.

John and Caroline left the house and went to yet another Christmas party. It was the same every year. Caroline always got drunk even though she dreaded the headache the next day. She always danced, but only alone, not with John or anyone else. John always danced with Kelly. Kelly had grown a bit more beautiful, Caroline thought. Her face glowed like the red Christmas lights were beneath her skin. Caroline wished she could wear a paper bag over her head. She thought of cutting Kelly's hands off with a sword.

John said he had something to do the next morning, so Caroline went alone to pick up Isabelle from his parents' house. When she got there, Isabelle ran to her and threw her arms around her legs. "Let's go, Mom," she said.

In the car she began to cry. "I want to go to my other grandmother's house," she said.

"Sweetie, your other grandmother lives in a different state."

She cried harder.

"What's wrong, Isabelle?"

"I don't want to go back there anymore."

"Why not?"

"I just don't."

"Did something happen?"

Isabelle pouted. She wouldn't answer.

Caroline knew something was not right. John's mother was crazy and so was his brother. John was sleeping with Kelly, probably even right now, while she picked up their daughter from his parents' house. Children could sense unrest, and Isabelle was unhappy. Soon Caroline and John would be divorced and Caroline would have nowhere to take Isabelle. She'd have to go back to work and pay for childcare, somehow. John would pay some child support. She wouldn't take Isabelle to John's parents' house after the divorce. It was too embarrassing.

Isabelle said again, "I'm going to cut off his hands and feed them to the alligators."

"Uncle Kyle's hands?" Caroline asked.

"Grandpa's hands."

Isabelle continued to ask about her other grandparents and continued to tell Caroline she did not want to go to John's parents' house and that specifically she didn't like her grandfather. Caroline never mentioned this to John, maybe because they were his parents and she didn't want to upset him. She didn't know exactly why she didn't mention it. It seemed it would take too much out of her to do it. Caroline stopped sleeping with John and John continued to sleep with Kelly, but he never spoke to Caroline about it, and she never asked him, she just knew. She never asked him about his parents, either. She never told him about the things Kyle said or the things Isabelle said. Kyle was just on drugs, and Isabelle was a child, she told herself. Isabelle was just an imaginative child and she was jealous that other children had two sets of grandparents around instead of one.

One Saturday night, Caroline got a phone call in the evening from John's mother. "Come get her," she said. "She's acting crazy." John stayed at the party and Caroline left. She'd only had two glasses of wine, whereas John had drank four and could not drive, he said.

When Caroline arrived, John's father was gone and so was Kyle. "Kyle drove him to the hospital," John's mother said. "Your daughter tried to cut off his hand with a knife."

"A sword!" Isabelle said. She was lying on the ground, rolling around and beating her fists against the carpet.

Caroline didn't even know Kyle could drive. "I am so sorry," she said to John's mother. John's mother crossed her arms over her chest and frowned. A pregnant Boston Terrier rubbed against Caroline's leg. Caroline didn't like the Boston Terriers. They were too small and sneaky. She preferred big, obvious dogs, if there had to be dogs at all. The pregnant dog went over to Isabelle. Isabelle got up and walked right out the door.

The divorce came, and then John's marriage to Kelly. Caroline went back to work, and she and Isabelle sold the house and moved to an apartment. Caroline hired a pregnant teenager to babysit Isabelle, and they never saw John's family anymore. Caroline thought Isabelle would give the teenager practice. John paid child support. He and Kelly moved to another state to be closer to Kelly's dying mother. Isabelle cried every day and saw her father once a year when they could afford plane tickets. She was seven, then eight, then fourteen.

Caroline never got another boyfriend or husband. Isabelle got a boyfriend and Caroline didn't like him. His name was Quentin and he made Isabelle cry because he told her he wished her hair was blonde instead of brown and that her breasts were bigger. When Caroline told Isabelle she thought Quentin was an asshole and she should dump him, Isabelle screamed that she loved him. Caroline found condoms in the bathroom and tried not to see pictures of Isabelle and Quentin in her mind, but she saw them. Caroline took Isabelle to the doctor to get birth control pills. Caroline hated birth control pills because of the side effects, and she hated that Isabelle had to take them just to sleep with her piece of shit boyfriend who probably only watched the misogynistic variety of porn because that was the easiest to find, and probably didn't even know or care what a clitoris was or where it was located.

Caroline's mother started to die, too. She took Isabelle to visit her. Isabelle wouldn't stop texting Quentin They seemed to be arguing. Isabelle's grandmother stroked Isabelle's hair and told her she was beautiful. Caroline could tell Isabelle didn't believe it.

At the motel, Isabelle sat on one bed and Caroline sat on the other. Caroline turned on a sitcom. Isabelle continued to text and started to cry.

"What's wrong?" Caroline asked her.

"Nothing," she said. She cried harder.

"Is it something with Quentin?"

"No!" Isabelle screamed at her. "You're always so mean to him!"

"I think he's damaging to you," Caroline said.

"You're a bitch," Isabelle said.

Caroline said, "I want to help you."

"You can't help me."

"But I want to."

Isabelle cried and went into the restroom. Through the door she told Caroline about things she saw when she was with Quentin. She said sometimes she saw the skin melt off his face until there was nothing but blood and bone. She said sometimes an army of spiders would march out of his mouth and cover this mass of blood and bone and try to crawl onto Isabelle.

"Oh, my God," Caroline said. "Please dump him."

"It's not his fault," Isabelle said.

Caroline put her hand on her knee. She wanted to stoke Isabelle's head, but she couldn't.

Isabelle came out of the restroom and got her sketchbook and a black pen out of her bag. Isabelle was a good artist, Caroline thought. Isabelle drew a picture of a boy's face stripped of skin and covered with spiders.

"Whose fault is it?" Caroline asked her.

Isabelle only glared at her, then went back to sketching her pictures.

Catherine remembered their conversations when Isabelle was little. She remembered that Isabelle had cried and repeatedly begged not to go back to John's parents' house, to have a different babysitter. She remembered when Isabelle tried to cut her grandfather's hands off with a knife. Catherine knew that she tried to cut his hands off for a reason. She remembered how she never told John, how she never said or did anything.

Caroline couldn't tell if the counseling and medication really helped Isabelle. It depended on the day. Caroline made a mental note that it would be better to teach men not to abuse others in the first place rather than trying to heal all the women after the fact. She thought making a mental note was not enough, but she didn't know what else to do. Sometimes Isabelle screamed at Catherine, and other times she was nice and let Catherine braid her hair while they watched *Mulan* or *Peter Pan* together. "I love you, Mom," she'd say. "Sorry I'm a pain."

"You're not a pain," Catherine would say. Isabelle would only look at her. There were things they did not discuss. There were things they lied to each other about. Catherine supposed this was normal when dealing with teenagers.

After a few months Isabelle broke up with Quentin, or he broke up with her. Either way, he was gone, and Caroline was glad. Isabelle didn't get another boyfriend. She started cooking for Caroline a couple times a week, and she also spent a lot of time in her bedroom drawing and listening to music that sounded like growling monsters.

John's parents died in a car crash. His father had been driving. They were coming back from the mall and it had started to rain hard. Somehow, he lost control. This didn't fit with Caroline's picture of him. She thought he never lost control. There was going to be a funeral, a military funeral where men wave flags and shoot guns to honor the veteran. John told Caroline he wouldn't be going. It was too far and expensive and his father was already dead anyway, plus he couldn't get away from Kelly. Things were bad with her mother, who was still alive and needed support. Caroline thought she should go to the funeral, to show respect, and that Isabelle should go too.

"I don't want to go," Isabelle said.

"But they were your grandparents," Caroline said. Caroline remembered going to her own grandparents' funerals, and how she hadn't wanted to go either. But it was just what people did. Funerals gave closure.

"I don't care about them," Isabelle said.

"They loved you. Your grandmother loved you."

"No, they didn't," she said. "And I didn't love them, not him or her. Just because you share blood with someone doesn't mean you have to love them."

"Isabelle!"

"Blood means nothing to me. It's stupid to tell people who they have to love." She went away to her bedroom.

Caroline wondered what would happen to Kyle. She thought he would die without his parents to care for him. He had no job, and she didn't know whether he'd be allowed to stay in that house or not. She wondered what would happen to all the dogs.

"You may be older now, but I'm still your mother," Caroline said, gently pushing Isabelle into the car to go to the funeral. She didn't know if she was doing the right thing; she never knew if she was doing the right thing. Parenting was impossible, especially alone. Isabelle looked out the window away from her mother. She put her headphones in to listen to the monster music.

When they were driving along the lake, almost at the cemetery, Isabelle took her headphones out. "When I take baths, I think about dying," she said. "I put my head under the water and hold my breath. I want to fall asleep in there and never wake up."

"Isabelle!" Caroline said.

"It's true," she says. "I want to die. I want to walk right into that lake and never come back out."

"You've been watching too many movies," Caroline said.

"Fuck you," said Isabelle. She looked out the window.

They drove up to the place where the funeral was going to happen. The army men already stood in a straight line with their neat hair, holding their guns upright like toy dolls. They were so still they looked dead. Isabelle rolled down her window to look at them better. "I hate the army," she said to her mother. "I hate wars. Killing people is wrong."

"Oh, sweetie," said Caroline. She remembered the graffiti on the wall from the Christmas party years ago: "I am a teenager. My life is the size of a walnut. I do not care about Afghanistan." This wasn't true about Isabelle.

To the row of army men Isabelle yelled, "I hate you!" The men stood still as figurines. Caroline remembered gardening when Isabelle was a baby. She remembered finding plastic army men under the ground, where some former little boy resident had buried them. "You should be ashamed!" Isabelle called to the army men. "I hate you!"

The men didn't look up. Isabelle was sobbing. Caroline saw Kyle standing under a tree, speaking to some people she'd never seen before. He was laughing. He didn't see her. Caroline continued to drive. She drove away from the funeral party. She drove all the way around the cemetery and back to the exit. She drove away. She drove herself and Isabelle all the way home and when they got back she stroked Isabelle's head and Isabelle let her.

THE HILLS

LENA AND HER GRANDMOTHER are taking a walk through the yellow hills when the grandmother drops to her knees, rustles her hair in the grass, and begins rolling up the hill. Lena has seen children rolling down hills, but never someone rolling up, especially not an old person.

"Grandmother, you're doing it backwards," Lena says. She chases after her. When she catches up, she puts her foot on the grandmother's back to hold her still. "I said you're like a backwards child."

The grandmother looks as if she doesn't remember what a child is. She often forgets things now, or remembers things incorrectly. She sometimes thinks she is a mermaid, or the widow of a handsome, famous baseball player.

"You remember children," Lena says. "Those very small people."

"How small, exactly?"

"Well," Lena says, looking around for an object the size of a child, but finding nothing but hills, "some are as small as a loaf of bread, even."

"And just as soft!"

"Maybe," Lena says. "Some are bigger. Some are more like a toy trunk."

Lena's grandmother picks a dandelion and runs her fingers up and down the stem, getting them green and filthy, Lena is sure.

"I'm a child," Lena says. Lena is eleven, so she is almost not a child, really, and she is a very mature and intelligent child. But she decides not to complicate the issue by explaining all of this to her grandmother.

"Ha!" says the grandmother, now chewing the stem. "I've never seen you roll down a hill in my life. That would be far too much fun for you."

Lena remembers when she was six, and her grandmother took *her* for walks, not the other way around. It's true, Lena never rolled down the hills. She didn't want to get grass stains. Lena wondered if the grass stains would be yellow, since the grass here always seemed to be.

"Grandmother, you really shouldn't chew on that dandelion."

"This isn't a dandelion. It's a puff globe."

"There's no such thing as a puff globe," Lena says. "That's called a dandelion."

"A dandelion, my foot! If this is a dandelion, what are those yellow ones?"

Lena ruffles her forehead. "Daffodils," she says.

"And I'm a child and you're a potato plant! Rubbish!" says Grandmother.

Lena helps her grandmother up, taking her hand so they may continue their walk. The doctors say it's important for the grandmother to get exercise, so taking her for walks is one of Lena's chores now. Lena moved here with her mother last week, just for the summer, probably, to help take care of her. Lena still has to do her normal chores—taking out the trash, feeding the fish, cleaning the windows—but she has to take the grandmother for walks too. While completing only her normal chores, Lena earned seventy-five cents per week allowance. Lena's mother refused to give her a raise for taking on this additional chore, on the grounds that the grandmother was Lena's grandmother. Lena found this unfair and noted that when an employee works extra hours, he or she is paid overtime, and so Lena should at least get a quarter for the extra time she would spend taking the grandmother for walks. Her mother told her she was a pain in the neck and stalked off.

Lena decides this walk has gone on long enough and that it's time to steer her grandmother in the direction of the house. Everything looks the same around here because it's the countryside. There are no other houses or landmarks in sight, just dried grassy hills, so Lena carries with her a compass she received for her eleventh birthday.

She reaches in her pocket for the compass, but finds nothing.

"Oh no," Lena says, hands patting down her clothes, "I must have dropped my compass."

"We don't need it," her grandmother says. "You think I don't know my way back? I've lived here my whole life!"

"I need to find it whether or not we need it to get back!" Lena says. "It was a birthday gift from my mother. I love it. I need to find it. And besides, you *don't* know your way back."

"The way back is up," her grandmother says.

"*Up* is not a direction," Lena says. "There's North, South, East, and West."

"Not at all! There's also circles, zigzags, down, and certainly *up*."

Lena sighs. She knows her grandmother won't see reason about this, so she just begins to rustle around in the grass in search of her compass.

"Are you looking for gold?"

"No, I'm looking for my compass."

"But there's tons of gold out here! I know your mother won't pay you an extra quarter for taking me on walks—"

"She told you that?" Lena asks, looking up. She feels a pang just below her sternum.

"But I've got tons of gold at the house! I'll give you a piece when we get back."

"*If* we ever get back," Lena says. "Everything looks the same here. It's all just dry hills."

Lena's grandmother gets the look again, like she doesn't remember what hills are.

"Oh, Grandmother, you remember hills," Lena says. "They're all around us right now."

The grandmother points to a fly.

"No, not those. Hills are large half-circles coming out of the Earth. Maybe the size of a shed. Or some are bigger, like several tractors put together."

Grandmother curls up on the ground like a cat. "I'm a hill," she says.

"No, Grandmother, you're a woman."

Grandmother points to herself and says "hill" so quietly Lena can barely hear it. Her eyes stare at nothing.

Lena continues to sift through the grass without moving too far away from Grandmother, who remains still as a barn owl. Lena swats a fly away from her face. She takes a few steps left, pushes the grass around, takes a few more steps left, swats away another fly. She digs and pushes and swats and steps left, needing to find the compass, needing for this walk to be over.

After several minutes Lena looks up and sees what must be hundreds of flies buzzing all around her. She swats one off her knee, then another off her T-shirt, then another off her other knee. As one takes off, another lands, and still another buzzes right up to her ear, so that she can feel the vibrations, as if they were inside her own head. She flails her arms in front of her as she walks forward in search of Grandmother. Could it really be that while searching for one thing, she had lost another?

"Grandmother!" Lena calls. "Grandmother!" But a fly buzzes into her mouth, and Lena bends over and spits onto the grass, wanting water, wanting chewing gum. She spits out the fly and calls to her grandmother again, but she doesn't answer. Lena begins running straight ahead, her arms knocking the stream of flies sideways and sometimes in zigzags. Then she remembers she took a lot of steps to the left, so she turns to the right and begins running that way, even though she is lost. But soon she hears a voice: "The way back is up!"

Lena turns around to see her grandmother, holding Lena's compass, which gleams in the sunlight.

"My compass!" Lena says. "You found it."

"The way back is up," her grandmother repeats, and begins once again rolling up the hill, the bones in her back and shoulders rattling.

"Grandmother, stop!" Lena says. "You'll get hurt! Your bones will crack like egg shells!" But another fly buzzes into Lena's mouth, and she again bends over, coughing and spitting onto the ground. Lena imagines her grandmother's insides as a network of bobby pins clipped together, threatening to snap apart should she bend a joint too quickly. Flies continue to buzz around Lena, and she swats them, and she can't get the taste out of her mouth, but she manages to say in a voice the grandmother surely cannot hear, "Grandmother, give me back my compass."

SLEEPWALKING

SLEEPWALKING BECOMES MORE DANGEROUS if you live near a body
of water. After midnight, when we'd all gone to bed in Marysville, Washington, a small town north of Seattle, our four-year
old daughter Maggie would sneak out in her sleep, wander across
the wet grass to the pond. I'd find her wading through the water,
the hem of her nightgown floating up with the waves, her hands
reaching out towards I don't know what. It happened often and
we feared it every night.

Of course we locked the doors, but sleepwalkers can fiddle
with locks. We put up a fence, but Maggie learned to climb it. She
was athletic because of the ballet lessons. Rachel called the doctor
and asked what we should do. "Nothing helps," she said. "Not the
art therapy, not the meditation exercises. And she gets *enough* sleep,
so it's not that. What are we supposed to do?" She'd pace back
and forth from the kitchen to the living room, running her fingers
over every surface of furniture and frowning at the dust, letting out
small puffs of air in between talking.

"Sleepwalking is often caused by stress or anxiety. You might
try avoiding any type of stimuli before bed," the doctor said. "No
television, no rowdy games. Try not to read her any stressful
bedtime stories, either."

"Last night I read her *Caps for Sale*," Rachel said. "It's about a man who sells caps. But he falls asleep against a tree, and when he wakes up, monkeys have stolen all his caps. He gets them back, though. Is that too stimulating?"

"I don't know," he said. "Did she sleepwalk?"

"Yes. She sleepwalks all the time."

"Then perhaps it's too stimulating."

Rachel had a problem with anxiety. She said this had to do with how much pressure she had been under as a teenager, when she was a highly ranked gymnast in a wealthy, WASP-y suburb of Boston. Her parents had hoped she'd attend a good college, then marry and/or become a senator.

I met Rachel in a bar a few months after she graduated from Tufts, a good college, where she'd studied Literature. She'd moved to Seattle where she'd gotten a job at a small publishing house. The job was actually an internship and it didn't pay a living wage, but it was good experience, so her parents supplemented her income. I was the same age as Rachel, but had not gone to college. I was waitressing, like I had been doing since graduating high school. I was at the bar with a male friend I was casually sleeping with. We both stared as Rachel spun alone in the middle of the floor. Actually, everyone stared. She was blonde and tanning-booth tan, and wore pearls and a khaki dress. I had short dark hair and mostly shopped at second-hand stores.

To my surprise, she approached me. "Do you know the actress Selma Blair? You look just like her. She is so beautiful." She touched my hair and flashed a big smile. I smiled back, no teeth though. I didn't like my teeth; they were a bit crooked.

I didn't know the actress. "Thanks, I think," I said.

"You're kind of like a character she plays in one movie. At first, she's quiet and rough around the edges, but then she turns out to be so nice and strong. I bet you're nice and strong too."

"I'm not sure about that."

"Oh, come on," she said, taking my hand. "Dance with me!"

I wasn't sure about that, either, but I liked her in a way I didn't usually like women. I wasn't sure why, because I didn't really like pearls or khaki dresses or Hollywood actresses. But I gulped down the rest of my beer and followed.

We went swimming in the lake that night, despite my concerns about getting in trouble because the park was closed. But she made me feel excited enough to do it. I was also worried about getting dirty, but she said "Who cares?" She kissed me on a bench beneath a pine tree. We went to her apartment, where we talked about Sartre. I had read a book of his, but didn't feel I really understood it. She seemed to understand everything about him.

"People think the existentialists are so negative," she said, pouring me more wine. "But they're not. They only say there is no *inherent* meaning to life. That doesn't mean there is no meaning. It means we are free to create our own."

"But what if we don't know how?" I asked. I thought to myself, for example, what if I am a waitress forever? I don't want to be and I personally don't find meaning in it. I didn't say these words to her exactly. "What if we can't create meaning, or we create a meaning we don't like? Then it's all our fault."

"Yes, it is. But that's the beauty of it. You can always go back and change it."

We slept very well.

A few days later we threw some things in the silver Prius Rachel had received as a graduation present and drove to the ocean. We went to a place where you could pitch a tent on the beach, so close to the sea animals. We thought it was funny to imagine fish sleeping. We talked about what strange things might live on the ocean floor, all the things scientists had not yet discovered.

After only a few months of dating we moved in together. Rachel said she liked our camping trip and wanted to move somewhere "in the country." How we came to live in Marysville specifically is Rachel had a cousin, Jennie, who was high up in the management at the nearby casino, and Jennie got me a job there waitressing (the tips were much better than at my previous job).

Rachel quit her publishing job because it was now too long of a commute. She did some freelance editing work from home, when work was available.

Jennie was too skinny in a coke head sort of way, and when she wasn't working, only wore black T-shirts with names of rock bands on them. It didn't make sense to me that she was related to Rachel, but Rachel said Jennie's parents were "different."

"I just don't understand why she sleepwalks at all," Rachel said on speaker phone with the doctor, once again, poking her head out the sliding screen door while Maggie drew with sidewalk chalk on the patio.

"It often happens when people are stressed or aren't sleeping enough," he said. "Try doing more quiet activities. Not so much stimulus."

"We live in the middle of nowhere in a beige house. She's four years old. How could she be stressed?"

"Children are mysterious," he said, which made Rachel huff out more air and fluff her apron to shake off all the bits of flour.

I had grown tired of Marysville. It wasn't a nice place. The grocery store was open twenty-four hours a day. The workers wore bright orange uniforms and rode around on giant beeping carts with extendable ladders, restocking the oversized, dented boxes of Cheez-it crackers and Cheerios. At yard sales, people sold used games of Clue and Monopoly for a quarter while bulldogs nipped at their muddy boots and denim pant legs. Rachel and I had been happy there for a time. The upside was, it was very cheap to live there.

"Jade, could you pick up some herbal tea on your way home?" Rachel would call, the phone cord braided through her fingers. "It might help with the sleepwalking."

Rachel stopped doing the freelance editing when she had Maggie (via sperm donor, via her parents' money). She wanted to spend time with her child. Some people didn't understand why the one with the college education stayed home, while I, who only had a high school diploma and no skills other than waitressing, worked. But that's just how it was. Also, she was an English major.

As for my parents, they had never been very involved. I was the product of a one-night stand and never met my father. My mother had kept me for a few years, while she still lived with her own mother, but then she moved out and left me there. My grandmother raised me until she died when I was seven, and then I went to stay with my mother's sister, my Aunt Sarah. I saw my mother occasionally, but she was rarely truly cognizant, due to drugs. So, my mother was not very involved, though she did make it clear that if I was a "dyke," I'd break her heart. I didn't speak to her anymore. I told her about Rachel. She had hung up on me and didn't answer when I called back. I stopped trying. I sometimes wondered about my father, but my mother couldn't remember his name.

Since the sleepwalking started a year ago, Rachel and I had grown farther apart. Rachel became consumed with it. She'd spend all day at home holding up calming, pastel paint swatches to Maggie's wall, cutting fresh flowers for her nightstand, skimming all her books and hiding the too-stimulating ones under our bed. She did all of this while Maggie wandered alone outside, doll in hand, throwing stones into the water or dragging sticks through mud. I spent all day at the casino. Originally, I had hoped I could move up to a better position there, but I remained a waitress. Rachel's failed cures for Maggie were becoming expensive, even in Marysville.

Rachel showed no signs of planning to work full-time. I would occasionally gently nudge her, but she didn't seem concerned. Because of her upbringing, she wasn't used to having to worry about money, and it's like she was incapable of doing it. I wanted to make enough that I could afford our current lifestyle, which was not even close to what Rachel was used to, but I couldn't. I had always been weird about money, not having ever had any.

"Listen, Jennie," I said one day on lunch break, "I really appreciate you getting me this job. But Rachel's spending all the money I'm trying to save buying herbal tea and yoga videos for Maggie. I might not mind, except none of it cures her."

"You need more money?" she asked.

I nodded.

"Look," she said, "I can't get you a promotion here. That's not how it works."

I nodded and looked down.

She sighed. "I do know a way you could make extra money, if you really need it, but you can't tell Rachel."

That's how I started working for the Mason family. I never did anything visibly illegal, though I was sure it all was. They'd ask me to go grocery shopping for them and to leave the car unlocked in the parking lot. There would be several large bags, whose contents were a mystery to me, in the trunk, and they'd be gone when I came out of the store. Or they'd ask me to buy something small with a hundred-dollar bill (probably counterfeit) and bring them back the change. Or I'd drive them places and wait outside, even though they could have driven themselves. They were easy tasks and the pay was decent, but I wasn't supposed to ask any questions or tell anyone about the things I did. I did these errands before or after my shift, raising little suspicion from Rachel.

The Masons looked normal and were very nice. They were a couple, Mr. and Mrs., in their forties. They offered me coffee and snacks when I went to their house. They had two very well-trained pit bulls and several grown children. Mrs. Mason called me "sweetie pie."

I hid the money I made in a small box in the tool shed. Rachel never went in the tool shed. I'd figure out what to tell Rachel once I made enough to make an actual difference.

Maggie would be starting kindergarten that fall, and asked me to take her to the school playground so she could know what recess would be like.

"Mommy," she said as I pushed her on the swing, "how did you and Mom meet?"

"We met after Mom finished college and we went swimming at night." I noticed a hefty man with a red beard standing near the edge of the playground, in the distance, who seemed to be staring at us. I narrowed my eyes at him.

"I like to go swimming at night, too," she said, her feet trying to kick at the woodchips below her, only they were too short. We went swimming at night and were stupid enough to think that was beautiful and would make us happy forever.

"You shouldn't do that," I said. "No, we did it when we were awake and much older than you. It's different."

"Okay," she said. The man in the distance began to walk off.

I took her to 7-11, and we bought Lemon Heads and some tiny airplanes made of foam, which we flew as the sun set.

About a month into working for the Mason family, I began to worry. I saw the same man with the red beard a few more times. At first, I thought it was a coincidence; Marysville wasn't that big and it was normal to begin to recognize certain strangers. But then it was too many times, and I always caught him looking at me. When he noticed that I noticed, he'd look away and leave. He came into the casino a few times, but didn't play any games or order any food.

I also began to wonder what was in the bags. They were large, but usually not heavy enough to be guns, not light enough to be marijuana, I thought. As I carried them from the Mason house to the car, it felt like trying to guess the contents of a Christmas gift.

One evening I decided to check. I had two bags to deliver that night. I knew I shouldn't, but I thought there would be no way they'd find out; it was my own car, it wasn't like there were cameras inside it. I pulled off into the parking lot of Maggie's future elementary school, which was empty this time of day. I climbed out and opened the trunk, and was ready to unzip the bag, first checking around to make sure I was truly alone. I was. Inside the first bag I found a lot of Styrofoam packing peanuts. As I dug through them, I found not guns or drugs but guns and drugs, what looked like cocaine. I re-zipped it.

The other bag was the same size but lighter. I unzipped it. Again, I found a large number of packing peanuts, but this time I found three smaller bags, each filled with what appeared to be a kidney. I quickly re-zipped the bag. My hands held onto the zipper tight, as if the bag might pop back open of its own accord. I got back in the car and drove off.

Probably the kidneys were not from murdered people, I thought. Maybe it was just underground market stuff. People selling their organs. I wished I had not looked in the bags. How could I keep working for these people now? Before, I had pretended it was all harmless, but now I felt implicated. Their cocaine was going to people like my mother, possibly ruining lives. And what if these people were mixed up in even worse things? What if I got caught and went to jail? But I couldn't stop working for them. Would they really let me just walk away?

"Jade, are you sad you never went to college?" Rachel asked me one night, climbing into bed.

We didn't discuss this often. "Yes," I said. "Yes, I'm sad. But I couldn't afford it, and it didn't seem that important at the time."

"What about your parents?"

"My *mom*?" I reminded her. "She didn't care."

"How could she not care? My parents forced college down my throat since pre-school. Either it would be a way to a good job, or a way towards a partner with a good job," she said. I frowned. "Oh, sorry," she said. "Anyway, I'm sure even if your mom wasn't around, she still wanted the best for you. And what about your aunt? I'm sure she did too."

"We lived in different worlds, Rachel. Their idea of *the best* isn't the same as yours."

"We're *from* different worlds, but now we live in the same world. The same house, even." As if those were the same.

"Okay, you're right," I said, pulling the blankets up to my chin. I didn't feel like getting into some big discussion right then.

"When did you know you were gay?"

"I'm not really gay, not like one hundred percent gay."

"Okay, whatever. When did you know you were bisexual?"

"I don't know. It's like I said before, I didn't think I'd ever be with a woman until I met you."

"But how can that be true?" she said. "You're straight as a pin, and one day you just meet me and soon afterwards decide you want to move in together?"

"Yes, that's what happened."

"How?"

"I don't get why it's such a big deal," I said. "I think people just fall in love. I think we just like someone, for whatever reason, and we gravitate towards them."

"I don't think so," she said, rubbing lotion on her hands. "I could never date a man. I mean, not after high school. Everyone always expected me to, since I was girly or whatever. And it's so hard to not act how you're expected to in high school. But I could also never date a Republican or someone who enjoyed wrestling."

"I dated a Republican man for sixth months and it was okay at the time."

"Do you even care that we have so much in common?" she asked.

"Like what?" I said, without thinking. Oops.

I guess we did have some things in common. I liked literature too. Just, I read Camus and Woolf on my own and probably didn't understand them properly, whereas Rachel's parents paid for some guy in a suit could tell her what it meant.

"Like, we both like dancing?" she said.

"That's true."

"We haven't gone out in forever," she said. "I feel so suffocated."

"You could get out more, you know," I said. "You don't have to stay home all the time."

"But I do have to stay home," she said. "Who's gonna take care of Maggie? We can't afford daycare." As if she really took care of her. She was always on the phone all day while Maggie played alone in the yard. "Maybe when Maggie starts kindergarten…"

"Let's go out this weekend," I said. "We'll leave Maggie with Jennie."

"Oh, yes," she said. "Can we please go? I love you." She kissed me, then turned away to fall asleep.

That Saturday, we drove Maggie to Jennie's.

"Mom, I don't want to go to Jennie's house," she said. "It smells weird in there, and her voice is too loud and too fast, and so are her dogs."

"You'll be going to sleep soon," Rachel said, lining her lips in the rear-view mirror at a stoplight. "You won't have to listen for long."

Maggie frowned.

"Come in," Jennie said, holding her bulldogs back by the collars, opening the door a crack.

"You want a beer?"

"Sure," I said.

"Jade, shouldn't we get going?" asked Rachel.

"Um," I said.

"I'm just gonna use the bathroom first." Rachel clinked down the hall in her heels. Maggie gravitated towards the television, which was playing music videos.

"So, how's everything going?" Jennie asked.

"I dunno. Fine, I guess. They give me money, and I don't ask questions." I wondered if I should mention the kidneys to her. I decided to play like I didn't know. "Do you know what's in those bags?"

"You can't ask what's in those bags."

"Is it drugs?"

"Seriously."

"Guns? Something worse? Any chance you know how I could stop working for them?"

"Jade, just drop it. It doesn't matter. Just keep plugging away," she said.

"But—"

Rachel returned from down the hall.

"Okay, Jennie, I brought some supplies for Maggie," Rachel said, her hands digging to the bottom of her purse, which was embroidered with her initials. "Some herbal tea for right now—not too soon before she goes to bed. A guided child meditation video—she can watch that while she drinks the tea—oh, she should probably stop watching those music videos, they're so hectic—some of her favorite stuffed animals, her own pillow with the ponies on it—"

"I think I can handle it," Jennie said, balancing the jumble of items in her arms.

"Great. You're the best. Ready?" she said, turning to me.

"Sure."

We kissed Maggie goodnight and drove to a dance club in nearby Everett. The club was small and kind of dingy, but it was something. And Rachel was right; we needed to get out.

"So," I said, "which one of us is driving home?"

"I can drive," she said. "In college I'd drive to an off-campus party, take four shots as soon as I got there, wait a few hours, and then drive home. It was fine."

"I guess," I said.

"Yep," she said.

And so we drank the shots, and then we danced. The club played popular eighties songs and projected the music videos on the wall. Rachel grabbed my hand and spun me over and over again. I still loved when she danced; even when dancing to these ridiculous songs, her limbs reminded me of branches moving in the wind. And her smile was different when she danced, more real.

I went outside for a breath of air. I went across the street, because there was a large group of men in motorcycle jackets who I didn't want to talk to outside of the club. I sat on the curb and looked up at the stars. I didn't know any constellations except the Big and Little Dipper. I bet Rachel did. Rachel knew everything and she was beautiful, and I was a fool not to love her.

Across the street, I saw the man with the red beard stomping out a cigarette. For what must have been a whole minute after he finished, he just stood there, staring right at me. Finally, he got in his car and drove away.

I was ready to leave the club when I went back inside. My buzz had worn off and I was over the Eighties music. Rachel had taken two more shots with strangers during the ten minutes I was outside, and had given them her phone number. She always flirted with men in bars, perhaps not because she liked them, but because she was pretty and thrived off making people happy and she felt it was obligatory. Still, I hated that she couldn't take me seriously enough to stay away from the men.

I drove too fast the whole way home to release some tension, but actually this just made it worse. Having little faith in Rachel's anti-sleepwalking regiment, I was still anxious about Maggie.

"Rachel," I said, "what do you think about 'thrownness'? The existentialist thing?"

"Oh, that's important. It means that even though we're free to create our own meaning and make our own choices, there are still certain things we are born into that we can't change, and that determine parts of our lives. Like each person is born with a certain race, sex, social class…"

"I know what it *is*," I said. "I mean what do you think about it?"

"I think it's important," she said. "I just told you."

"Well," I said, "how much can we overcome? Is there a limit? Just like for example, in my own life, how much freedom do I really have?"

"Don't you think you've already overcome a lot?" she asked.

I didn't answer. Rachel fell asleep in the passenger seat and we drove the rest of the way in silence.

"Jennie," I called into the living room when we arrived at her house, "how's it going? Where's Maggie?"

"Oh, hey, guys!" Jennie said. "Back so soon? Did the club suck? It is Everett, after all. Maybe one of these days we can go to Seattle—"

"It was fine. We had a good time in spite of it all. Where's Maggie?"

"Okay, jeez. She's in my room, sleeping in my bed, while I sit out here watching *The Price is Right* and waiting for you to come pick her up so I can go to sleep. You're welcome."

"I'm sorry, Jennie. I'm just stressed. I didn't mean to sound ungrateful. I really appreciate you watching her."

"Okay, yeah, no problem." Jennie turned her head away from me, back to the TV.

Jennie lived on a small lake.

I went to her room and switched on the light. No Maggie. I went outside and ran towards the water.

"Jade, where are you going?" Rachel called after me, holding her shoes in one hand. "Wait, I'm coming!" She followed me, barefoot in the mud.

I saw the red-bearded man wading in the dark water. The lake flopped calmly as his big legs moved. Maggie was next to him. "Maggie, what are you doing?" I ran to them, and Rachel caught up with us.

"Mommy! Hi. We're swimming!" She wasn't asleep.

"Maggie, get away from him right now."

"He's my friend, Mommy."

"What are you talking about?"

"I met him the other day while I was playing in the backyard. Mom was on the phone inside. He said it would be easier if I didn't tell her."

"Maggie, you should always tell me *everything*," Rachel said.

"Rachel, take Maggie inside," I said.

"Who is that man?" she asked. "Jade, do you know him? Who is—"

"Rachel, just do it."

She did it.

"Look, lady, you should really stop working for those people," he said.

"What were you doing with my daughter?" I said. "And why have you been following me around?"

"She said she wanted to go swimming. I didn't see a problem with that."

"But what were you doing?" I pulled out my cell phone. "I swear I will call the police right now. What are you doing here and what were you doing in my yard the other day?"

"Just doing my job, lady, okay? Just like you. Put that phone away, you know you can't call the cops. I know about you."

I put the phone down, and pulled out a knife that I carried with me these days. "Tell me who you are, you fuck."

"Oh, a knife, you really think I don't have a—" he patted his pockets. "Oh. I really don't have anything." He hit his forehead. "Stupid!"

"Talk to me."

He sighed. "Okay. If I tell you the truth, will you promise not to tell anyone?"

"Will I promise? Are you in third grade?"

He sighed again. "Honestly," he said, "I'm supposed to bring her down here to scare you. Same thing with following you around. They know she sleepwalks by the pond and you have a thing about her drowning now. Except you weren't supposed to see me. I was supposed to leave her down here and put a note

in her pocket that said, 'We are watching you.' And somehow
I was supposed to make it clear that I meant the people I work
for are watching you, not the people you work for. Honestly, I
hadn't gotten far enough to figure out how to make that clear.
Also, your daughter was supposed to be asleep, but I had to
knock on the bedroom window to get her to wake up and come
outside. I managed to get your daughter outside without that
other lady noticing, but you two got back too soon. I'm not
very good at this job. But don't worry, I wouldn't really let her
drown or anything."

"Don't worry?"

"Look, I'm sorry. I'm just trying to make money, like you. I
have a kid too, and a wife. So, what do you say, I won't tell if you
won't tell?"

Rachel stomped back out of the house. "Jade, what the fuck?"

I sighed. What to say to her?

"Oh, hello, ma'am!" said the red-bearded man. "Nothing to
see, nothing to worry about here, just a slight misunderstanding."

I sighed again. "Rachel," I said, "okay. I'm sorry. I've been
working for some people to make extra money, just doing odd
jobs, you know. I want to make enough for us and for Maggie,
to help her stop sleepwalking and for you to have the things
you want."

Rachel frowned, then smiled, then frowned. "You mean, are
you like cleaning houses or something?"

"Well, not exactly."

"What does this have to do with this guy?" she asked.

"She's working for basically the mafia," he said.

I turned to him. "What the fuck!" I said. "Let me explain to
my own wife!"

"Look," he said to me. He sat down on a log. "What are you
doing? Your daughter is clearly neglected or something, you're
lying to your wife," he said, gesturing at Rachel, who was fuming,
"when really you're working for these terrible people, I mean

that's a pretty big deal, and it doesn't seem like your relationship is all that healthy, and you leave your daughter with this crazy lady who didn't even notice she was no longer in the bedroom."

I glared at him.

Rachel glared, then slapped me.

"I'm sorry," I said.

She stormed off, back into the house.

The man pulled out his pack of cigarettes. "Do you smoke?"

"I guess," I said. He lit mine, and we sat on the edge of the water.

"Why'd you do it?" he asked.

"What?"

"Move in with her and have a child. Why'd you do that? I mean, you're not even a lesbian, right?"

"How do you know what I am?"

"I told you, I know about you. That's what we do."

"Okay, well, first of all, I'm not a *lesbian*, but...I mean I never thought I'd date a woman, but then I fell in love with Rachel. Big deal."

"Yeah, that's what I mean. You're not a lesbian."

"Okay, whatever," I said. "I don't know why I did it. I guess I didn't have anything else going for me. And I wanted things to change for the better."

"So, you moved to Marysville?"

"Well, we lived in Seattle originally. But then we had some idea about how we hated people and nature was beautiful so we just came here. And Rachel's cousin was here and could get me a job."

"Um, Marysville isn't really the best place for nature lovers," he said. "Or lesbians. You should go to Boulder or something. It's kind of shitty here."

"How did you start working for the mafia?"

"I don't work for the mafia. I just told you to stop working for them, remember?

I work for the other people, like the anti-mafia, the good guys. Or at least, the better guys. Still illegal I think. But I kind of just fell into it. It doesn't matter. I love my family and I love my life. The difference is, you don't."

"Do you really think you know the first thing about me?" I asked. "I love my daughter more than anything. And I love Rachel. She's beautiful, and she's so much smarter than I will ever be."

"That's not true," he said. "She's just educated. Rich people always seem smarter. They talk fancy, and they know a lot about food, enough to ask for special things at restaurants, like undercooked meat and lemons in their water. And they have all those long books on their shelves. But have they even read those books? I doubt it."

"Rachel has," I said.

"Just think about it," he said. "Your life, I mean. You're still young. You don't have to do this forever."

"That would be nice," I said. It would be nice for Maggie to get better. It would be nice to get a different job, something I liked. It would be nice to live somewhere else, maybe Seattle after all...did I *really* hate people? Did Rachel? And it would be nice for Rachel to look at me sometimes, just hold my hands in hers and look at me and love me, because I didn't really hate her, I just hated certain things about her. Because I was jealous.

"As for what's in the bags," he said, "there's guns and drugs, but also organs. But don't worry, they don't do murders, not anymore. It was too risky. My people gave them trouble. It's just the organ trade."

"You say I should stop working for them," I said. "How do I get out of it?"

"You just leave," he said. "They'll never want to let you go. They'll do anything to keep you. But you have to try. It'll be easier if you move far away, and never, under any circumstances, tell the cops anything. Just leave."

We shook hands, and he started to leave, but turned back.

"It's like you're sleepwalking yourself."

The rest of my life can go one of two ways.

No, of course, it can go more than two ways. It can go more ways than I can imagine. For example, I never imagined to live in Marysville, but here I am. But for now, I can think of only two truly conceivable possibilities, only two ways out of the place I am now.

Possible Life Number 1:

I never see the red-bearded man again. I put Maggie in psychotherapy and make a point of playing outside with her each day after work. Sometimes we go swimming, while we are awake. All the exercise tires her out so that her body cannot possibly want to swim at night, though she might still sleepwalk. Perhaps it is not the absence of stimuli she needs, but the presence of the correct stimuli. Somehow, with the help of Jennie, I undo my involvement with the Mason family. Maybe I hear from them once in a while in the future, maybe I get a call or see one of them watching me from the edge of the playground, the edge of Maggie's college campus. But they never hurt us. They just keep tabs.

I think about the red-bearded man on occasion. I consider leaving Rachel and going somewhere else. Maybe Colorado. I think about working in one of those ski resorts at a nice restaurant where people tip a lot. I could meet someone else, maybe someone who understands the first thing about me. I consider leaving, but I don't actually leave. I watch Maggie as she completes her first kindergarten homework assignment, which is to draw a picture of her mother, and she has two, and I know she will have her first experience of bullying as soon as she shows it to her classmates.

I call my own mother. I talk to her one last time. She won't die immediately afterward, but she won't forgive me for what I've done, marrying a woman. What I've done.

And what she did to me, I won't do to Maggie.

Possible Life Number 2:

I seriously consider leaving Rachel, and I do. I don't love her. Rachel moves back to Boston, with Maggie. She gets Maggie, because she is the birth mother and that's what the court cares about. I see Maggie when I can. I do move to Colorado and work in a nice ski resort restaurant. I meet someone else. I love that person, maybe. If I'm lucky. At the very least, I can stand that person, and I like some of the things they do. We enjoy some of the same activities, and we have fun on the weekends. I move up to management at the restaurant so I can make more money and see Maggie more often. I get old. Some other things happen, such as new friendships and hobbies.

But:

There is a third way my life could go.

This is only if I can be really brave. But it is also my best shot at happiness.

To achieve this life, I will have to admit to myself a series of truths, all of which scareme.

1) My father does not matter. He never did, and I have nothing to gain by thinking of him.

2) My mother does not matter, either. She gave birth to me, and I am grateful. They say you should love and call your mother, no matter what. But this is not true, not for me.

3) I am not actually stupid.

4) I am more than just a victim.

5) All those things Rachel said about existentialism, she was right. I can change. We can change. We can move.

6)   Maybe what Maggie needs is a change of environment, not a yoga video.

7)   Maybe what Maggie needs is her mothers.

8)   I can understand existentialism, and I always have. I understand lots of books.

9)   There are things that I like. There are things that I dislike. For example, I like to read, and to write, and to think. I like children. I want to be a teacher, and I always have.

10) I can still go back to school. I can still become a teacher.

11) This will take a lot of work, and some logistical and financial reorganizing. But I can do it.

12) Rachel is not evil just because she grew up rich.

13) Maybe I can teach her some things, too. If I only open up to her.

14) What my mother said about being a dyke, it doesn't matter.

15) Did I ever have a boyfriend I loved more than Rachel? I did not.

16) I have wasted time. But I still have more.

17) When I see her, my body relaxes, even now. Something breaks inside of me, but it's something that needs

to be broken so that something better might grow there.

18) I really do love Rachel.

19) I really do love Rachel.

20) I really am capable of love.

THE PAPER GARDEN

I WAS NEVER ABLE to remember the names of flowers. I could only remember those names that also have other meanings: bleeding hearts, bluebells, foxglove. My mother had all of these in her garden and when I helped her in the yard I'd only want to water those, not the other flowers. My mother humored me for a while, thinking this was cute, thankful for the help, even planting extra bluebells for me. She watered the other flowers. But as I got a little older, this was no longer cute; it was silly, then irritating. I tried to tell her I didn't like doing things I didn't understand. It would be like saying words in a language I didn't know or letting a stranger into my bedroom. She jerked the watering can out of my hands and said then *go play your games inside.*

Around that same time, that summer when I was eight, something happened between my mother and father that I didn't understand, something that changed my mother, making her sad and a bit mean, and we had to move someplace else without Dad. This new place was an apartment complex that had a pool but didn't have a garden or any space to make one. Sometimes I'd hear my mother whispering and sort of crying into the phone in the middle of the night, but I'd pretend to be asleep, because I knew that if I went to her, it would only make things worse. When I cried about missing my dad, she only cried harder.

One morning shortly after moving there, I went over to the window and carefully peered behind the curtains, keeping my whole face hidden except for my eyes. Outside I saw a girl a few years older than me holding something long and thin like a cigarette. Two smaller girls, maybe her sisters, rolled in a square of dirt like baby pigs, laughing. She said something to them that I couldn't hear, then rolled her eyes and turned away. She seemed to think they were idiots, and so did I.

The older girl's name was Leah. She was ten, but she was the closest child to my age in the apartment complex. We became friends. The smaller girls were her sisters, five-year old twins. Leah liked to abuse her sisters in any way she could think of, because they were younger and it was easy. The twins were always around, because Leah's mother made her take them everywhere. It was as if Leah was a babysitter, although she was not a very good one. Sometimes I thought the twins would be better off if they had no babysitter at all.

Leah stole cigarettes from her mother's purse and smoked them. The twins realized stealing was wrong, but they didn't realize it was a problem for a child to smoke. "Give back Mom's cigarettes!" they said to Leah. "You didn't ask first!" The twins' names were Morgan and Emma, and they were not identical.

"Quiet," Leah said, pushing Morgan down with her foot. "She wouldn't share if I asked her to. I'm only taking what's coming to me." I wondered how old you had to be to get cancer.

Every time Leah and the twins came over, my own mother would crinkle her nose like she smelled something bad, but she must have assumed Leah stunk because of her mother's smoking. She kept letting me hang around her.

Once, we all walked to 7-11 to buy candy bars, but when we got there, Leah turned out her pockets to demonstrate she had no money. She shrugged and took three candy bars and put them in her pockets.

"Bad Leah!" the twins said. She shoved the twins and they shut up.

"Um," I said. I turned out my own pockets and found the dollar my mother had given me. It was only enough for one candy bar. "We could share?" I said. Leah laughed like this was a stupid idea. She walked out of the store and the twins followed. I went up to the counter to pay.

After the twins ran back inside and told on Leah for stealing, her punishment was to pick up all the cigarette butts in the parking lot of 7-11. I helped her. "You don't have to do that," said the man who worked at the store. That man always seemed to be there no matter what day or time it was, and he spoke very quickly like he was a wind-up toy than never ran out of energy. It was hard to imagine him sleeping. "It wasn't you who did it," he said to me.

I shrugged. I felt guilty even though it had been Leah. I would have felt guilty if I'd told on her or if I hadn't. I didn't know what I should have done. The twins sang songs and ate the candy bars while Leah and I picked up the cigarette butts. Leah said, "This blows." Every time she found a butt that was only half-smoked, she put it in her pocket to save for later. "At least there's one good thing that came out of this," she said.

When I got home, my mother said my hands smelled like cigarettes and she asked me why that was.

"I just helped to pick up all the cigarette butts in the 7-11 parking lot, that's all," I said.

"Why would you want to do that?"

I shrugged. I couldn't tell her about Leah stealing, or she might not let me hang around her anymore, and I had no other friends in this place. "It was Leah's idea," I said. "She wanted to do something nice for the neighborhood."

"What a strange thing to do," my mother said, then bowed her head to say grace.

That night I heard Mom crying once again, so I decided to make her a garden of paper like the garden we had at our old house. I set to work with my scissors and crayons and I folded the flowers, placing them in a line right next to her armchair: bleeding hearts, bluebells, foxglove. I hoped she would love it, even if they were a little crooked.

The next morning I noticed other paper structures next to the ones I'd made. I had no idea what they were. My mother said they were the other flowers, that I had forgotten some. She walked out of the room. I looked closer and still I couldn't see what she meant. I made another foxglove, this time a fox wearing a glove, plus a church bell that was blue, plus a human heart that was bleeding. But I didn't do a good enough job making that one, so I threw it in the trash.

I never told Leah about the paper garden, because I knew she'd think it was stupid baby stuff. Leah was tired of kid things such as art projects and board games. She liked adult things like smoking and setting fires.

It was hot and the twins brought a water gun and Leah brought one of those long lighters used to light candles in jars, and we went into the woods behind the apartment complex. Leah told the twins they couldn't squirt the water gun until she gave the word, which was fine with me because I didn't want to get wet. There was a creek back in those woods and we walked until we found it. The twins tried to catch water bugs, but they weren't fast enough. Leah took the squirt gun from the twins and they cried.

"Hannah, hold out that lighter," she said, handing it to me. I held it out. "Now light it," she said.

"Why?"

"I want to watch this water put out the flame."

I shrugged. I held the lighter out as far away from my body as I could get it. I lit the flame. Leah squirted the water gun and the flame erupted into a fire the size of a baby. Its flames spread across some little sticks on the ground. "Wow!" Leah said. She jumped up and down with happiness.

I rushed over and threw as much water as I could cup in my hands on the fire. Then I did that over and over again as fast as I could. The twins did it, too, but Leah just stood there laughing at the flames. The three of us worked until the fire was out, then Leah stopped laughing.

"How did that happen?" asked one of the twins.

"I filled your water gun with gasoline," Leah said.

While we walked back, I asked Leah why she hadn't told me about the gasoline. She said, "Because if I told you, you wouldn't have gone along with it."

A month went by and it was still summer and I hadn't seen my dad since we moved out of our old house.

"Where's Dad?" I asked Mom.

She glared, not at me but just in general. "He's with Nikki," she said.

"Who's that?"

"She's his new woman."

"What do you mean?"

"You know what I mean," she hissed.

"Can I go see him?"

"Why don't you ask him?" she said.

"I don't know where he is."

"He's at our old house, Hannah."

"Oh." I still remembered the phone number, which Mom had made me memorize in case of emergencies.

I went out of the living room and got the phone in the kitchen and dialed. It rang and rang and there was no answer. There was no answering machine, either, although we used to have one. He must have turned it off because on the old answering machine, it said all our names, and now it was just him who lived there, and maybe this new woman Nikki, whoever she was.

I went back into the living room where Mom was sitting in her armchair. I climbed into her lap. "You're getting too big for that," she said, staring out the window and not looking at me. I climbed out of her lap, then I took her hand and kissed it like I was a gentleman. I went and got my paper and scissors because I decided to make some ladybugs for the paper garden. Paper gardens were a great idea, I thought, because the flowers would never die, not even if it snowed. Everybody should have a paper garden, even those who lived in houses like our old one with Dad.

When I had a sleepover with Leah, her mother made us take a bath together even though I didn't want to. "This is how we do it in our house," she said. "Leah always takes baths with her sisters, and you are no different." She left the bathroom, mumbling something to herself. The twins weren't in the bathroom with us, probably because four people would be too crowded for one bathtub.

Leah took off her clothes like it was no big deal, then got into the tub. "Come on," she said. "We're both girls."

I carefully removed my clothes and put my arms across my private areas. I scrunched my body into a little ball when I got into the tub. Leah splashed me. "Come on!" she said again. She stood up and she spread her private area open like a blooming flower, another kind I didn't understand. She wanted to show me something but I didn't want to see it. "Let me see yours," she said.

"No way."

She wiggled around like she was dancing.

"I don't want to," I said.

She sat back down and scooted closer to me. She plugged her nose and plunged her head under the water and tried to touch me in my private area, then by reflex I jammed my knees together on her head. She jerked up and screamed "Ow!" When her mother came running to the door, Leah told her I hit her.

Her mother glared at me. "Are you okay, Leah?" she asked.

"I'm okay, Mom."

"Good." She went out of the bathroom.

A few weeks went by. School would start soon and I'd have to go to a new school, since we moved to a new district. We hadn't moved that far and I didn't see why I had to go to a whole new school but that's what Mom said. We went school shopping to buy the supplies on the list my teacher sent and Mom sighed and said it was too expensive, but bought the things anyway. Any time adults talked about money that summer, it made me sad, no matter what they were saying.

Dad finally called. He picked me up and took me to Chuck E. Cheese and gave me a twenty-dollar bill when it was over. "I had fun with you, Hannah," he said on the drive home. "We should see each other more often."

"Yeah."

"I'm sorry I've been so absent." When children are absent, it means they skipped school. When adults are absent, it means they're bad parents. Dad didn't use to be so absent when we all lived together. He used to help me build forts.

"Why did you and Mom get divorced?" I asked.

"It's hard to explain," he said.

"Is it because of Nikki?"

"How do you know about her?" he asked. "Did your mother—"

"Yes."

"No, it wasn't because of Nikki." I knew he was lying.

"Does she live with you now? Is that why we went to Chuck E. Cheese instead of our old house?"

"Well—"

"I don't like her."

"Hannah, you haven't even met her."

"I don't care."

When we got to the apartment complex, I got out of Dad's car without saying goodbye. I slammed the door quickly so I wouldn't hear him say goodbye either.

In bed, I wondered why I could stand up to Dad but I couldn't stand up to Leah. I told Dad I didn't like Nikki but I could never tell Leah I didn't like her. Maybe when I went to the new school I'd be so busy with my homework that I wouldn't have time to spend with her. Mom said they give kids more and more homework these days. The year before, I did have a lot.

One day Leah asked, "Hannah, do you know what sex is?" I'd heard the word but I didn't know what it was.

We were sitting on her bed. She said sex was when a man and a woman lay on top of each other and do disgusting things. I got a bad feeling in my stomach like I was going to throw up. "It's what your mom and dad did to make you come alive," she said. "Now it's what your dad does with Nikki."

"You don't know anything about that," I hissed.

She asked if I wanted to do it, but I said neither of us was a man so how could we do it? She said she could be the man. I said no thanks. I got up to leave. She said, "Wait!" but I didn't wait.

Dad called again and asked to see me. I was tired of the same old people so I said that would be fine. He picked me up and took me to our old house.

Nikki was there. She looked younger than my mother, but not as pretty in my opinion. "I'm Nikki," she said.

I said, "I'm Hannah. I'm eight years old, and I used to live in this house."

She laughed and turned to my dad. "She's so cute!" she said.

Dad ordered pizza and we ate together. It was strange eating with this new woman at our old table where we used to eat meals with Mom, who cooked them. Mom always cooked delicious things. I did like pizza but I liked it better when Mom made it.

"I work at Cinnabon at the mall," Nikki said. "I love cinnamon rolls, but they're so bad for my diet." I thought one good thing about Nikki was that she could get me free cinnamon rolls, maybe. I also thought that pizza probably wasn't good for her diet either.

"Yeah," I said.

"What do you want to be when you grow up, Hannah?" she asked.

"I want to be a singer. I want to be so famous that everyone gives me free stuff just because they love me."

"But you're so shy," said Dad.

"I am not shy," I hissed.

After we ate we played Go Fish. I won every time because they let me. They thought I liked this but I didn't. I was getting too old for things like that.

When I got home, I told Mom that Nikki was okay but not as good as her. Mom said, "Well, tell that to your father." I said I did tell him. Mom started to cry once again.

The day before school started, Leah and the twins and I went into the woods once more. Leah had asked me to bring my Barbie doll, which I thought was strange since she didn't like kid things and Barbie was definitely a kid thing. The twins had no water gun and Leah had no lighter this time, so I didn't feel so afraid.

Once again, we walked until we found the creek. The twins jumped up and down in the water, getting their clothes and shoes wet and muddy. I felt sorry for their mother, who had to clean up after them all the time. I tried to be very clean to make things easier for my own mother. She was sad enough all the time as it was.

Leah grabbed a big stick in her hand. She pointed it at the twins. "Now, take your clothes off," she said.

Morgan said, "but this is not bath time."

Leah said, "take your clothes off."

"But what if someone comes?" Emma asked.

"Nobody's coming."

"But what if they do?"

Leah pointed the stick and glared at them. "If you don't take your clothes off, I'm going to bash your heads in with this stick." It was a really big stick.

The twins screamed.

"Shh," said Leah.

The twins got out of the stream and took their clothes off, then stood there shivering.

"Hannah, take your clothes off too."

"No," I said.

"Hannah, if you don't obey me I will bash your head in with the stick."

I shook my head. "No," I said. She glared. The twins shivered. Leah came over to me and yanked the Barbie out of my hands, then took her clothes off, then threw her on the ground and stomped on her.

"That's what I'm going to do to you," Leah said, "if you don't obey me."

I shook my head again. I looked at the twins and said, "you can put your clothes back on. She's not going to hit you."

The twins didn't put their clothes back on.

"Now," she said to them, "stand closer together. Face each other." The twins obeyed. She said, "rub your bodies together."

"Ew," they said.

"Do it!"

They did it and began to cry.

"Stop!" I said. "She's not going to hit you. Please stop doing that and put your clothes back on." They just cried harder.

I went over to Leah. I pushed her and took the stick from her. "You can stop now," I said. "I have the stick." Leah picked up another stick.

"Take your clothes off," she said to me, "or I will hit you." I stood there. I went over to the twins' clothes and picked them up off the ground, then started putting their shirts back on over their heads. They struggled.

Leah came over and hit me in the face with the stick. It stung bad. She hit me again and a small piece of wood got into my eye. Tears came even though I tried to keep them away. I didn't want to be a baby. Leah kept hitting me with the stick until my face bled. The twins cried harder.

Leah put her hands under my shirt and tried to pull it off. "No!" I yelled. She yanked it off.

Then I took her stick and hit her in the face several times. I took my shirt back and ran away.

Back at home, I told my mother what happened. I told her Leah was trying to make the twins have sex and she was trying to make me do it too. My mom asked me how I knew what sex was and I said Leah told me. She asked how she could try to make us have sex and I told her it was complicated. I also told her about the time in the bathtub and the time Leah stole the candy and all the cigarettes.

Mom washed up my face and got the piece of wood out of my eye. I looked in the mirror while she stood behind me. There were slash marks on my cheeks and my eye was red and terrible. "Great," I said. "My first day at the new school, and I look like a monster."

Mom kissed the top of my head. "You're not a monster," she said. She took me to my bed and read me a story. I realized I'd forgotten my Barbie doll in the woods. Usually I slept with her next to me. Mom went into her closet and got the stuffed dinosaur I'd loved as a baby.

"Mom," I said, "I left the twins out there with Leah."

"It's okay," she said.

"What if Leah killed them?"

"She didn't kill them."

"What if she made them have sex?"

"I'm sure she didn't do anything like that," Mom said. But I knew she did something bad. I shouldn't have left. It was like I did it as a reflex.

Mom went into the living room and brought back a few flowers from the paper garden. She set them up in a vase on the nightstand and she got into bed with me. Mom said, "you didn't do anything wrong." Somehow hearing her say that was worse than if she had said I did do something wrong.

After that, Mom said I couldn't hang around Leah anymore. Once in a while I'd see her swimming in the pool or just going in and out of her apartment, with the twins trailing behind her like baby ducks. She always avoided my gaze and pretended not to see me. I couldn't help but stare at her and the twins. I wanted to see if they were okay, and figure out what would become of the three of them. The twins still acted the same, sticking their tongues out and singing and sometimes slapping each other. They'd wave at me and call out, "Hi, Hannah!" and they'd point to me and ask Leah "Why do we never see her anymore?" and Leah would just say "Who?" and keep on walking.

I started at the new school and I did have a lot of homework. I told myself it was so much that I wouldn't have been able to see Leah even if she had been a nice friend. I told myself it was so much that I wouldn't have been able to see my dad even if he had been present. I did my homework extra slow on purpose. My favorite subject was science, where I got to learn about new animals and plants. I got very good grades.

Even though I had no time for friends, I did have time to add to the paper garden. I now had a produce section with carrots and strawberries, plus some spiders and butterflies, plus a section for everything I learned in science.

But sometimes in the night, I'd cry like a little baby.

Years later, because of the good grades, I got a scholarship to a good college across the country. It was so far away that I had to take three flights to get home for my Christmas visit. That first year, it was snowing so much at the good college that my first flight was delayed for twelve hours, and I didn't sleep. When the plane finally left, we headed for Atlanta.

During my layover in Atlanta, I saw a girl of about ten bossing around a pair of twins about five. I thought of Leah. I hadn't seen her in at least eight years, since Mom and I moved out of that apartment complex into a better one. I never knew what had become of her, or the twins. I wondered what all Leah did to them while I wasn't there, and if they were traumatized now, if they were maybe into drugs or would get into drugs in the coming years. I wondered if Leah was into drugs, too. I was into drugs, but I still got into the good college and thought I had a shot at a nice life.

The ten-year old girl and the twins began hitting each other, then an adult appeared behind them and said, "Stop it, or we'll go back home right now!" The twins stopped. The adult turned away and the ten-year old pinched the twins in the ears. The twins looked at me as if asking for help, but I just looked back down into my book.

SNOWFLAKE

ONCE THERE WAS A pregnant young woman, a queen, who wished she was not pregnant. "This baby will ruin my body," she said. "My breasts will sag, my stomach will balloon. I'm not ready to ruin my body. I'm only seventeen years old." She'd been having sex since she was married at thirteen, but this was the first time she'd gotten pregnant. Her husband the king was away most of the time, fighting wars and conquering lands. The baby kicked inside her, imitating this violence. The queen took her appearance very seriously, so much so that she owned a talking magic mirror from whom she sought affirmation twenty-four times a day. "Magic Mirror," she would say, "who's the fairest of them all?" The queen had white skin. She equated whiteness with beauty and with general superiority.

"You are the fairest of them all, my queen," the mirror would say, every time. The mirror had a man's face and a man's voice. The queen would smile, and then the mirror's man-face would fade away in order to reflect her own, which, she had to admit, was quite beautiful. Her lips were red. Her eyes were emeralds. Her hair was long and black as night. She wore elaborate dresses in purple fabric, and diamond earrings like stars against her black sky of hair.

The queen had gotten pregnant from having sex with one of her servants. Her husband the king was always away. He wanted to get as much land and money for himself as possible. The queen could not care less about conquering other lands. She wasn't even allowed to leave the castle grounds, anyway, so what did it matter? Hundreds of guards with automatic weapons roamed the castle and its grounds, making sure the wrong people didn't get in or out.

The queen felt that she barely even knew her husband, so she didn't feel too guilty for sleeping with the servant, who happened to be very handsome and very interested in the queen. She and this servant got along quite well. Plus, she was sure her husband had had dozens of girls, pillaging foreign villages and whatnot. The queen did not take birth control pills because of the acne, weight gain, and depression.

Of course, the servant refused to wear a condom. Men say they can't come anymore unless they're raw-dogging. Some men can't come anymore unless they're watching porn. They could have the most beautiful girl in the world, but they need a machine, hundreds of girls on screen with bleached blonde hair, plastic surgery, and waxed assholes being pounded and hammered and doubly penetrated by penises the size of small dogs, all while screeching with pleasure. Erectile dysfunction has become an epidemic in young men, unable to be stimulated by anything "less" than a high-resolution video of a BDSM orgy full of three-titted cyborgs.

"Will I be replaced by a sex doll?" the queen wondered. "Perhaps a sex robot?" Lots of people have already been replaced by machines. Mostly peasants. Peasants are poorer than ever these days.

Even though she was the queen, she had no real political power and she wasn't allowed to make any new laws. The legal ban on abortion that her grandfather's grandfather's grandfather had instated centuries ago remained intact.

The queen was not about to let some peasant shove a wire coat hanger into her womb for a hundred bucks. Of course, that's what the peasant women did when they found themselves in trouble. Half the time those procedures resulted in injury or death, since those performing the procedures were not doctors and did not exactly know what they were doing. The queen did not wish to die among peasants.

She could not leave the castle grounds to enter the witches' forest, so she used her magic mirror to summon a witch into her bedroom. The witch was hideous. The queen loved to be around hideous women. They made her feel great about herself.

"Can you kill what grows inside me?" the queen asked the witch. "Do you perhaps have some sort of potion?"

"I don't know any abortion spells."

"That is outside my skill set. I mean, I could cut it out of you just like anyone else, but that would leave you disfigured, plus you might die."

"Fuck!" said the queen. "You worthless, ugly hag!"

The queen shooed the witch away. "And never come back!" she yelled.

She carried through the pregnancy while her husband stayed away at war. He never even knew she was pregnant. He stayed away so long. The queen grew large and hideous. She hid herself inside her room, sobbing and clutching the magic mirror. "Who's the fairest of them all?" she asked.

"You're the fairest of them all, my queen," said the mirror.

"Even with my big belly?"

"Even with your big belly," said the mirror.

The queen stopped sobbing. She smiled, then stared off into space. Her mind was a cloud. Five minutes later, she began sobbing again, and asked the mirror "Who's the fairest of them all?"

"You're the fairest of them all, my queen," he said. And then a pause. "But, alas, something is about to change."

"What?" gasped the queen. She began to hyperventilate. "My body? What will the damage be, mirror? Will my breasts sag? Will my stomach remain ballooned, even after the baby is gone?"

"No," said the mirror. "You will give birth to the child. Your body may look slightly different than it did before, but not much. That sort of thing doesn't matter. But this child, this child, will change your life forever."

"What are you saying?" asked the queen.

"You're still the fairest of them all, " said the mirror. "For now." The Queen felt her heart do a somersault. "But when she comes of age, your child will surpass you in beauty. Then she will be the fairest of them all."

"It can't be!" said the queen.

"Oh, I assure you, it can."

The girl was born in a bloody mess. The queen sobbed the whole time. "She's ripping me!" she wailed. "I'm ripping in half!" Eventually, miraculously, it was over, and the queen was not dead. The cord was cut and everything was cleaned. They took the baby away and the queen went to sleep.

The next morning the midwife stood above her, holding the baby and smiling stupidly. "Would you like to hold her?" she asked.

The queen shrugged. The midwife handed the thing over and the queen carefully examined its face. "Hmm," she said. This baby didn't look like anything special. She looked like a regular newborn, that is, bald, rat-like, and rather ugly. But still, to be safe, she would have to dispose of the girl. The magic mirror was never wrong. He had never been wrong before.

That evening, the queen wrapped the baby in a blanket and tucked it under her cloak, so that it looked like she was alone. She went into the courtyard.

"Good evening, my queen," said a guard. "Shouldn't you be getting to bed? You'll need your beauty rest, your highness, after what you've been through."

"Thank you. I just came out for a breath of fresh air, that's all. It helps me sleep. I'll go inside in a few minutes."

"As you wish," the guard said, and he bowed. The queen knew they'd be watching her from a distance the whole time, making sure no harm came to her, but also making sure she didn't try to escape.

She went to the edge of the woods, to the stream that marked the border between the witches' forest and the king's castle grounds. She was not allowed to enter the woods. She used her cloaked body as a shield and placed the tiny black bundle in the stream. "You will drown here," the queen whispered. "They say you're hard to kill, but I know better. Babies are helpless." The baby stared back and didn't fuss at all. The queen frowned. "Or if you don't drown, you'll starve. And if you don't starve, the witches will find you, kill you, and cook you in a stew. A human baby is helpless and useless as a heap of shit. You'll never survive." The baby blinked her sparkling eyes, fluttered her long lashes. The queen spat. "Stay off my turf, you little cunt." Then the queen turned around and went back into the castle, wishing the guards sweet dreams as she passed them.

A baby girl was floating down a stream, all alone. She had no possessions and no one in the world to care for her. The baby was very, very sad. She didn't know what else to do other than to just keep letting the stream float her along.

After a while night turned into morning and the baby girl found herself deep in the forest. She came upon a family of foxes. "Oh, please," she said to the foxes. "Can you adopt me and be my family?"

The foxes looked at her with sadness and said, "We're sorry, little girl, but we're already so poor. We can't afford to feed another mouth." Animals and children can understand each other, if the circumstances are dire enough.

The baby continued floating down the stream until she came upon a family of deer. "Oh, please," she said. "Can you take care of me and be my family? I'm only a baby, and I have no one and nothing."

The deer looked at her with tears in their eyes. "We wish we could help you, little girl," they said. "But we're so poor, we don't even have enough to feed ourselves." The deer were very thin, she saw now.

She floated on. Eventually the stream ended, and she arrived at a cottage. "Someone must live here," she thought. It seemed like no one was home. Perhaps they were at work. The baby decided she'd rest here for a while, and see if anyone came home and took pity on her. She was very tired, after all. Babies must get plenty of beauty sleep.

Seven tiny men were walking home from the mines when they found a baby sleeping on their front porch. "What in the devil?" said one of the men, Hurly, their leader. They all stopped in their tracks, and were very quiet. None of them had ever seen a baby this young before. They all lived together in one house, and slept together in one queen-sized bed. They had no idea how to approach a baby. They had always thought babies were a women's issue. Was it dangerous? Would it bite, perhaps?

"Where did it come from?" asked Sneezy.

"Does it have a note?" asked Biscuit. He went up to the baby and examined her. He shrugged in order to indicate to the others that there was no note.

At this point the baby woke up. "Hello!" she said.

"Ack!" said Biscuit. He jumped. "It speaks!"

"I don't believe it," said Gopher. "We've found ourselves a baby genius."

"I need help," said the baby. "Would you please adopt me and be my family? I have no possessions, and no one to care for me. I'm also very, very hungry. I haven't eaten since yesterday afternoon."

Dopey grinned, and hopped inside to get her some milk. The rest of the men had a private huddle so they could decide what to do about the baby. They made sure to get several meters away so the baby couldn't hear. Gopher said, "Guys, I think we could make a lot of money off of this. This baby is a magic wonder.

People will pay to hear her talk, she's such a young baby."

"Rubbish," said Grumpy. "It's not that impressive that she can talk. Pretty much everyone learns to talk eventually, even animals. Plus, babies get older. Pretty soon, her ability to talk won't seem remarkable in the least."

"You're so heartless, thinking only about money," said Sneezy. "She's just a baby! We have to adopt her, or she'll die." Then he sneezed.

"Who cares?" said Biscuit. "She's not our responsibility. We can't just adopt every hungry thing that shows up on our doorstep."

"She's the only hungry thing that's ever shown up on our doorstep," said Window. Window was the wise one and everyone knew it. That's why he was called Window, because his mind was clear as glass. He saw everything as it was. "I think she needs us."

Dopey returned with the milk and fed it to the baby. "Thank you so much!" she said. "You are too kind."

Dopey blushed. He hopped over to the group of men. Dopey was a mute. He understood what others said, but he didn't speak. Instead, he gestured with his hands or acted things out as if playing charades. Occasionally he would write words in the dirt to Window. The words were not in regular language, though, it was a special language between Dopey and Window that no one else could understand. None of the men knew for sure if Dopey was actually unable to speak, or if he simply chose not to. A lot of trouble could be avoided by never opening one's mouth, it's true. Dopey pretended to be holding a baby, rocking her to sleep with a big smile on his face. He jumped up and down with joy and did several cart wheels in a row. He scooped the baby up and kissed her forehead.

"Oh, thank you!" said the baby. It was the best day of her entire life so far.

Seven years later, the queen stared into her magic mirror. Her

husband the king had died at war, and she had gotten a new
husband, a prince from some other kingdom. He was a mediocre
person, just like her other husband. He never said anything interesting. All he cared about was conquering lands, plus spreading
his religion all around the world and squashing out all the other
religions until his was the only option and everyone was the same
all over God's green Earth. The queen couldn't think of a more
pointless way to spend one's time.

She turned to her magic mirror. "Tell me, my darling," she
said, "who's the fairest of them all?" Even though she had aged
seven years and was now twenty-four, past her prime, she was still
incredibly beautiful, and the mirror told her she was the fairest of
them all every time she asked, just like always.

"Hmm," said the mirror. He scrunched up his face like he was
thinking hard.

"What?" said the queen. "What is it?"

"She lives," said the magic mirror. "She lives, and she is beautiful. She's the fairest of them all."

"She lives?" yelled the queen.

"Yes."

"Fuck!" yelled the queen. She picked up a candlestick and
threw it across the room. It shattered. The queen loved breaking
things and making messes, then forcing other people to clean up
after her. "But wait," she said. "You said she would surpass me in
beauty when she 'came of age.' If she lives, she's only seven."

The mirror shrugged. "Still."

"Jesus," said the queen. "That's disgusting." She used the
mirror to summon a forest witch to her bedroom.

"I can tell you where the child is," said the witch. "You must
walk into the forest, follow along the stream where you placed the
baby seven years ago. Follow the stream to its very end. There,
you'll find a cottage. Seven men live there, and your precious
Snowflake."

"Snowflake?" said the queen. "What sort of pussy name is

that?"

The witch shrugged. "The men named her. Anyway, you can go there. Disguise yourself if you wish. The child may remember you, and sense that you intend to harm her. Go there in the daytime, when the seven men are at work in the mines. Trick the girl into opening the door. She's only seven, after all. She's probably pretty dumb. When she opens the door, you shoot her in the heart!" The witch pumped the trigger of an invisible machine gun.

"Hmm," said the queen. "Okay. You will lead the way."

"Well, actually, tonight us witches have a ritual where we sacrifice animals to Satan, so I sort of had plans—"

"We're leaving now."

The witch sighed. "Very well," she said. In some situations, it seems clear who has all the power.

The queen had been trained with firearms because her husband thought it was necessary. She needed to know how to protect herself, in case someone broke into the castle and killed all the hundreds of armed guards who were supposed to protect her and then it was just her versus the intruder. The queen and the witch went to the armory and took two machine guns plus extra bullets. The witch enchanted the guards so they wouldn't stop the two women from taking the guns or from leaving the castle grounds and entering the witches' forest.

They walked along the stream. "Aren't you scared to be entering the witches' forest?" the witch asked.

"Pff," said the queen. "No. I have guns. Don't witches have to recite some long, poem-y spell in order to kill someone? With this gun, I just pull the trigger and BAM. It's all over." The queen laughed. Guns really were quite absurd.

"Anyone can get a gun in this kingdom," said the witch. "You think witches don't have guns?"

"What?" said the queen.

"It's legal for everyone to have guns. You can buy them at the store like a loaf of bread, as long as you aren't a child or a convicted felon."

"Hmm," said the queen. "That doesn't seem reasonable." The queen loved owning so many guns, but she did not like the idea of other people being allowed to own them. They could shoot someone! They could shoot her. Guns were way too much for common people to handle.

The witch shrugged. "I don't make the laws," she said. "That's your husband!"

It was true. Perhaps later, when the queen was finished shooting and killing her daughter, she would write to her husband about the possibility of changing the gun laws. Perhaps he'd be happy to see her show an interest in government, for once.

"Well, you'll protect me, won't you?" the queen asked the witch. "They won't shoot me if I'm with you, will they?"

"Of course not," said the witch. "I was just teasing. You have nothing to be afraid of."

The queen smiled.

At dawn, they arrived at the cottage. "We must wait until the little men leave," whispered the witch. They hid in the bushes until the seven men paraded out of their house and down a path to the mines, carrying their picks and singing about finding treasures. Except the last one in line. He wasn't singing, but he was dancing around stupidly to the tune of the others' voices.

"Do they really think they're going to find treasure?" said the queen. "If there were any treasure in these woods, wouldn't the king or the witches have found it by now?"

"These men are simple creatures, my queen," said the witch. "Look at their house. It's pathetic. They need to keep their dreams of riches alive, otherwise they'd have nothing to live for."

The queen nodded. She supposed if she were a peasant, she'd be the same way: either suicidal or else completely and willfully deluded about how things work.

"The witches allow these men to stay in our woods because they amuse us," said the witch. "They pose no threat to us. They are too stupid. We leave them alone, and they us."

"Okay, whatever," said the queen. "Now, let's go get her."

The witch cast a spell on the queen so that she looked like an old, ugly hag instead of a beautiful woman. This way, there was no chance the girl would recognize her mother. The hag queen got up and knocked on the door, while the witch waited in the bushes, watching. "Is there anyone home?" called the hag queen. "I'm just a poor old woman, lost in the woods! I'm quite hungry and tired. Could you help me, please?"

Snowflake's seven fathers had instructed her not to answer the door for any old, ugly women, because these woods were full of witches. Although the witches did not harm the little men, they weren't sure how they would react to a beautiful child. Children were one of witches' favorite things to eat. Snowflake's seven fathers had also instructed her not to answer the door for any beautiful younger women, because it could be her mother trying to kill her again. If her mother ever found out she'd survived, she'd be out to get her, for sure. So basically, Snowflake was supposed to be suspicious of all women, unless they were prepubescent girls like herself.

"I'm sorry, ma'am, but I'm not supposed to open the door for any old women," Snowflake said. She stood next to the door, her hand clutching the lock, as if some puny piece of metal would protect her from a witch intent on child murder.

"Why, I'm not old!" said the hag queen. "Don't you know it's rude to call a woman old?" The hag queen pretended to sob.

"Oh, please don't cry," said Snowflake. "I didn't mean anything by it. If it makes you feel better, I'm not supposed to open the door for any beautiful, younger women, either."

The hag queen continued to fake-sob. She devised a plan. "Well, if you won't let me in," she said, "will you at least open the window and pass me some food?"

"I don't know," replied Snowflake. "What if you try to grab

me?"

"Well," said the hag queen, "I'm just an *old woman*, remember? I can't possibly be very strong!"

Snowflake supposed the old woman had a point. Her body was thin and wobbly like some little twigs tied together, like you could snap her in half easily with a shoe.

Snowflake went into the kitchen, got some bread, berries, and deer meat and put it all on a plate. She filled a cup with wine. That's what everyone drank in this house.

While she was preparing the meal, the hag queen got her gun ready, and hid it behind her back.

Snowflake went back to the front room and opened the window to give the food and drink to the old woman.

The hag queen swung the machine gun out from behind her back, aimed at the girl's heart through the open window, and opened fire. "Die, you little bitch!" she screamed. Blood spurted everywhere like the grandest confetti. The girl fell over with a thump, and the hag queen fired the rest of her round through the open window just to add insult to injury, breaking glass and several objects inside the house.

"Yes!" yelled the hag queen. She tossed the machine gun aside, jumped up and down with joy. "I'm the fairest of them all! I'm the fairest of them all!"

The witch came out of the bushes. "You don't look so fair to me," she said.

The hag queen had almost forgotten that the witch had disguised her as an ugly old hag woman. "Oh, right," she said. "Change me back at once!"

"I'm afraid that won't be possible," the witch said.

"What?" said the queen. "Oh, no. Oh, no, you don't—" The queen went over to her machine gun and picked it up. The witch promptly aimed hers at the queen. The queen's gun was empty. She couldn't get the extra bullets from her pocket and load the gun. The witch might shoot her at any sign of movement.

"Throw the gun aside," said the witch.

The hag queen complied.

"Sit down."

She did.

"Now," said the witch, "this is how it's going to be." Suddenly, the witch transformed into the spitting image of the queen how she used to be, the fairest of them all.

"No!" cried the queen. "That's me!"

"Not anymore, it's not," said the witch queen. She cackled. "Imagine how powerful I'll be, with this beauty and my sorcery. It's simply fantastic. I'll enchant all those guards and do whatever I want! As for you, my queen—oops, I misspoke. You're not the queen anymore, are you?" She cackled again. "Well, I suppose I'll just leave you here to do as you wish. I could kill you, but I kind of like this better."

"What?" said the hag. "Do as I *wish*? What can I possibly do? I have nothing, and these woods are full of witches!"

"You'll fit right in," said the beautiful witch queen.

"You'll never get away with this!" said the hag. "I'll find my way back to the castle, and tell the guards the truth!"

"Ha!" said the witch. "First of all, good luck finding your way back. I'll enchant the stream so it leads you somewhere else. You'll never get back. And even if you did, do you really think they'd believe you? They'll think you're just some witch. They'll probably have you executed. Especially if I tell them to. Which I will."

"Curse you," said the hag.

"Well," said the beautiful witch queen. "Goodbye, then." She walked away, carrying the machine guns and all the queen's things with her.

All the hag had left was a pocketful of bullets, a broken plate of dirty food, and the clothes on her back. She sat on the steps of the little men's cottage, wondering what to do next.

The seven little men were taking their lunch break. Every day they each packed their own small picnic to eat in the middle of the day. This refueling was necessary, because working in the mines was hard physical labor.

Dopey had forgotten his own lunch on this particular day. Even though it was a simple task that he performed on a daily basis, he sometimes still forgot to do it. Dopey fluttered around to each of the other men, making eyes and silently begging like a puppy. But none of the other men wanted to share.

"Dopey, you're so stupid!" said Grumpy. "How could you forget your own lunch? You love to eat!"

Dopey shrugged.

Grumpy said, "Why don't you just go home and eat there? Then come back when you're done. Or don't come back. I don't even care! Just get out of my sight."

"Yeah, Dopey," said Biscuit. "Why don't you just go home? You can help Snowflake clean the house and cook our dinner!"

The other men giggled. They often made jokes meant to emasculate Dopey.

Dopey pouted. He turned around and followed the path home, angrily kicking little rocks as he went.

When Dopey got to the cottage, he saw that the window was broken and smeared with blood. An old woman was asleep or dead on the front steps. Dopey rushed into the house to find Snowflake. He saw her immediately, a red mess on the floor under the window. Her face was covered in a veil of broken glass. Dopey brushed the glass aside, causing more cuts. He winced. Her head was grossly disfigured and full of holes, her cheeks gone, teeth showing like a wolf's, eyes open in terror, no eyelids left, blood matted in her hair. Tears fell from Dopey's face onto Snowflake's dead skull, washing a very tiny amount of blood away.

Dopey went into the bedroom, into the closet where the seven men kept their seven guns. He grabbed his shotgun, then went outside to where the old woman was sleeping. He nudged her with the gun until she stirred and opened her eyes.

"Oh, no," she said.

"Mm—" tried Dopey. He hadn't spoken words since he was a child. It was not in his nature to speak. He did not like conflict. He preferred to express himself through actions, through hugs and giving presents and doing favors for people. Finally he managed to say, "Who you? Did you kill?"

The woman shook her head. "No, please—" she whispered. Dopey could see she was struggling to speak, too. He looked at her hands. There was blood on them and it reminded Dopey for a moment of beautiful red tulips and then the moment was over and he saw only blood and the blood on Snowflake's head from being killed and how her eyes couldn't shut and she couldn't put her teeth away and she was hideous so hideous he hated that he had thought of tulips just now seeing that blood.

Dopey screamed. He looked up at the sky and fired several shots in the air. The old woman jumped up. "Away!" yelled Dopey. The old woman started to run. "Leave!" said Dopey. He collapsed on the ground and wailed.

Later, after the other six little men had come home from the mines and found Dopey outside wailing and waving his gun, after they had gone inside and found the corpse, after they'd covered it and moved it outside, after they'd cleaned up the blood and the broken glass, Dopey sat outside on a log with Window. Window was always the best at comforting Dopey, being the wisest.

"Do you want to tell me how you feel?" Window asked. "You can write it in the dirt."

Dopey shook his head.

"Well, if you ever want to," said Window, "I'm here."

Dopey looked into Window's eyes and patted him on the knee.

"Well," said Window, "would you like to help me write a poem?"

This was a game they played. They always made the first two lines the same, and altered only the last two. It was Dopey's favorite game, but he would only play it with Window. He didn't like to even write words to the others. With Window, writing was okay.

"Roses are red," said Window, as always.

As always, Dopey wrote in the dirt with a stick, "Violets are blue."

"Things don't always turn out the right way," said Window.

Dopey wrote in the dirt with a stick, "But sometimes they do."

ACKNOWLEDGEMENTS

Thank you to the editors of the literary magazines in which some of these stories originally appeared:

"Tulips," *The Literary Review*
"A Red Winter Shadow," *The Rupture* (formerly *The Collagist*)
"The House," *Maudlin House*
"Doctor's Office Paperwork," *Entropy* (BLACKCACKLE Series)
"Pheromones," *Bodega*
"The Hills," Bad Pony:
"The Paper Garden," *Washington Square Review*
"Snowflake," *Whiskey Island*

Thank you to 7.13 Books and Hasanthika Sirisena for publishing and editing this collection.

Thank you to the English & Creative Writing departments at Colby College, Syracuse University, and the University of Louisiana at Lafayette. Thank you to my teachers: Jessica Alexander,

Adrian Blevins, Patrick Donnelly, Arthur Flowers, Skip Fox, Jennifer Geer, Natalie Harris, Peter Harris, Sarah Harwell, Brooks Haxton, Sadie Hoagland, Mary Karr, Christopher Kennedy, John McNally, Laurel Ryan, George Saunders, Bruce Smith, Dana Spiotta, and Debra Spark.

Thank you to the many people who gave me editorial feedback on earlier drafts of stories in this collection. Thank you also to my friends, family, and teachers for providing support and enthusiasm, which is where I found the ability to keep writing. Thank you Jess Acosta, Katie Baxter, Nana Adjei-Brenyah, Hannah Chapple, Chen Chen, Brent Daly, Martin Fulmer, Becca Shaw Glaser, David Gustavson, Cate McLaughlin, Mei the cat, Diane Michels, Erin Mullikin, Casey Nagle, Lindsay Norville, Patti Pangborn, Jess Poli, Jessica Scicchitano, Tyler Stephens II, Em Tielman, Ali Ünal, Bill Vance, Jane Vance, Vivian Vance, and Gina Warren.

ABOUT THE AUTHOR

Caitlin Vance is the author of the poetry book *Think of the World as a Mirror Maze* (Stubborn Mule Press, 2019) and the chapbook *The Little Cloud* (dancing girl press, 2018). Her stories and poems have appeared in *Tin House*, *The Southern Review*, *The Rupture*, *Washington Square Review*, and others.

www.ingramcontent.com/pod-product-compliance
Lightning Source LLC
Chambersburg PA
CBHW050142110726
47898CB00008B/2633